COLD

SPOT

by

Lou L. Berthelson

George Please Enjoy [signature] June 2017

This book is a work of fiction. Any references to historical events, real people, or real places and events are the products of the author's imagination, and any resemblance to actual events or places or persons, living or dead, is entirely coincidental.

Copyright © 2017 Lou L. Berthelson

ISBN 978-1544132358

Acknowledgements

Writing a book is a big job and impossible to do alone. I would like to thank all of those who made this book possible. Margo Huff, Sammy Soyring, Don and Laurie Cartwright, Glennetta and Mary Berthelson and my wife Tamara.

Dedication

To my wife Tamara who is the ultimate warrior and the love of my life. Also, to the memory of Sergeant Molly Malone of the Los Angeles Drug Enforcement Unit.

Prologue

1875 Coast of Maine

Shivering in November's midnight air, Sea Captain Norlander's wife Ruth searched the darkness from the widow's walk atop her house. She began to curse him and his travels when she saw it; then others appeared. They were slowly working their way out of the inlet this side of the Jameson light station. She hated it when they came; local lore says they are lost souls from shipwrecks, her pastor said they're demons; she thought they came with the house.

There were six of them tonight. Yellowish forms, smoke or cloud like, gliding across the water and then on to her property. If there were six of the yellows, then the others would be close. Ones you couldn't see, but she knew they were there. She could barely make them out. These aberrations caused black spots or holes in the landscape. It was as if they were pieces of black fabric floating through the night air. She could not see through them, nor see anything in them; like a black speck that crosses your eye; either way she knew these things were evil and they wanted in the house.

She hadn't remembered them coming this late in the year. Then she realized, the captain usually returned at the end of the summer months. They were not so bold when the Captain was home, but lately she had found that the doors had been strained against their locks. The strike plates and jams had been stressed to the point of breaking. The carpenter who checked the doors, told her to alert the constable to the likelihood someone had tried to break in.

Maybe stay with friends? No, she would stand her ground as the Captain had done. She would remain on her watch throughout the night, and not yield. She had thought it over. These things would not risk it with someone watching. She braced herself and whispered, "Ruth Norlander will stand". She could sleep during the day when they had retreated.

It grew much colder as the morning grew closer. She gathered more blankets around her and decided to sit. She could still see the ghostly yellow images glide along just above the surface. Strangely they would disappear into the ground, only to pop up many yards further ahead. She figured sun up in another hour.

Ruth could only find one of the black ones. Extremely tired she thought maybe she was imagining it. She turned to the right, to adjust herself to stand. Slowly realizing she could not see down the walkway, she looked left and could see the entire left side of the widow's walk. Disoriented, she turned back and everything went black.

Fear grabbed her entire body like a vice. Never had she been so afraid so fast. A stench like a rotting corpse filled her nose and lungs. Completely locked up by fear, she lost all emotional control. Suddenly it felt like she had been incased in ice. Ruth was helpless as the cold reached for her soul, screaming in her mind, she couldn't muster a whimper. With her entire body burning from the cold, she blacked out.

Later that morning the carpenter and constable came round to check on her. They found her in a chair in the middle of the widow's walk. It was upsetting to see the anguish on her face. Constable Dodd figured she had died from exposure during the night. The Carpenter didn't agree. It smelled like death all round her body; that should not have been the case, she was frozen solid as a block of ice

Chapter One

Present Day

Day One

1:00am

Dream Room,

Hart Compound

Jonesborough, TN

John Hart was sitting on the edge of his bed with his elbows on his thighs, and his head down almost between his knees. He was vomiting into a two hundred and fifty thousand dollar Ming Dynasty chamber pot.

Spasms from the dry heaves were causing him to panic; they had to relax if he was ever to breathe again. The fact John was going through all of this again put him in an extremely foul mood; he was not a nice guy when he had totally lost his temper. Molly, his German Shepard, was watching from the bed across the room; she could tell this was an extremely bad one tonight.

John Hart was a six foot two inch, strongly built, quivering mess. His dark brown hair was soaked black with sweat; his dark brown eyes were glazed over with tears. His facial features were taut and anguished, but would be best described as Scandinavian.

John knew he was in trouble. It was the retching part that really pissed him off, thus the expensive chamber pot. In the past John would throw the bucket, waste basket or whatever and destroy what he could around him. Besides making things worse, it just left him a nasty mess to clean up. John's girlfriend Kat bought the Ming for him six months ago; so far he hadn't thrown it.

As his spasms slowed John, stood up for a few seconds, and then started toward the shower. Trying to walk was not a good idea. As the vertigo hit, John's eyes were now darting back and forth uncontrollably; they made it seem like the room was spinning and rocking. It felt like he was falling down an elevator shaft really, really fast.

John had been through this several times before; slowly squatting down while reaching for the floor with both hands; he thought of crawling back to the bed; as he touched the floor the south wall video monitor came to life.

The rapid beeping of the alarm synchronized with the rocking of the room, as did the blinking of the red light. Someone or thing had set it off; John now cursing, screaming at the monitor, "What the hell is this now?" While trying to stand, John blacked out.

At 2:50am. John stirred a little; Molly's nose was in his ear; then her big paw on his chest. John not quick to rise, Molly lay across his stomach and licked his chin. Startled, John got her off of him, rolled so he could see the south wall; the monitor was still on; the alarm light was green. "Son of a bitch, really; what the hell is going on? This is the fourth time in two weeks. I thought it was fixed" He fell back flat on the floor; he looked at Molly, "I need lots of coffee." Molly barked; *we're going for a ride.*

Molly was not your everyday looking shepherd; she is what they called a Sable. The sables have two colors of hair over their bodies. Molly's was black over ninety percent of her body, with a silver coat underneath the black one. She was smaller than most shepherds, and her disposition was termed "soft". Prior to becoming an empathy companion, Molly was Sergeant Molly Malone of the Los Angeles Drug Enforcement Unit.

John was assigned Molly as his empathy dog. She was trained to help him in times of stress; she was a

Godsend. John was supposed to return her after he learned to cope on his own; instead John bought the company five other dogs and kept her. She had saved him at least three times a month for several years now.

John slowly made it into the shower. Now was when the depression would start. His shrink told him to review his blessings and victories as the depression came; she was a smart lady.

His dreams were similar, if not identical, to the horrible dreams experienced by hard drug users, or an alcoholic's delirium tremors during withdrawals. They were full of gore and unspeakable things. John's dreams were extreme in that they were in color, and included tastes and smells.

Tonight's dream, the second of three, featured hundreds of severed heads floating by the boat dock on which he stood. The slowly rocking, moored boats were filled with body parts; the heads had the faces of people he knew; the dock was surrounded by a lake of blood. This time one of the faces had been Chris Sims' his friend and the curator of the Hart Compound.

The most extreme part of the dream that launched him into consciousness was when all the faces suddenly turned and spoke evil things and mocked him; they hated him for being alive.

All of his three dreams were different, but they individually stayed the same; they came in a cluster each month. In dream number two sometimes the faces changed; nothing ever changed in the other dreams.

At first his doctors told him the dreams would fade as the drugs got out of his system; they didn't. The shrinks wrote it off to PTSD and offered drugs to deal with the situation; John refused.

John's recurring dreams were caused by past parental abuse; physical and emotional; which left him psychologically damaged.

The abuse was inflicted by his mother and several doctors whom she worked with in the Foster Care System. She would give John drugs that would make him appear emotionally or physically impaired.

The more John was impaired the more money his foster mother would receive from the state to provide for his care. She was using John to extract thousands of dollars a year that she would spend on herself.

She would pay more attention to the side effects of certain drugs than she did how they would help John. She was always looking for side effects she could turn into cash. None of her fellow workers or employees ever brought her to task.

Then, when John was seventeen, a Special Education Councilor at his high school called a meeting with a California State Foster Care Official and John's mother. He asked the state official to verify the medical diagnosis that led to each prescription. John's mother was given three months to produce the evidence or face a full investigation. She stalled until it was evident she was avoiding her fate.

After the meeting John's councilor spent many days with him formulating a plan they called, "Eighteen and Out". When John turned eighteen, he executed the final part of the plan.

He contacted a legal firm that had previously won a large settlement against the School district John was in. His councilor acted as his advocate and he sued the state of California, his mother, the school district, and several doctors.

They sued for one hundred million dollars and settled for sixty-three million. The suit had lasted three years until John's team finally proved his dreams would be with him his entire life, at that point the state decided to settle.

In 2006, at age twenty-one, John received the sixty-three million dollars. In the years following; by selecting the right friends and colleagues he had parlayed his settlement into a diversified fortune. He had people everywhere.

He was dressed, in old, comfortable jeans, a long sleeve gray Henley style t-shirt and pale timberline lace up boots. John had "almost hair" it was almost black, it was almost three inches long, almost styled, and he almost gave a shit about his hair. John turned his focused on the dream room; another blessing.

He designed the dream room just for these monthly occurrences. It was a large room with vaulted ceilings. The walls were a pale blue, ceilings light grey and there were beds on opposite sides of the room. There was an open shower stall between the beds on the west wall. There were three half walls forming the shower, with handicap hand rails inside and out. The entire floor was covered in hospital vinyl.

He stood enjoying the eastside view through five, thirty inch wide Georgian style, two over two, glass doors, topped with a curved transom with sun veining. He could see the front of the compound and the glow from the city of Jonesborough far in the distance. He liked what he saw; it looked like victory.

Chapter Two

3:30am

Hart Compound

John and Molly left the bedroom and headed toward the stairs that emptied into the great room below. John hung a left; Molly started getting excited. After walking about fifteen feet, on the left wall was what looked like a big linen closet; it was actually the elevator down to the lab level.

All the underground facilities were accessible from a main tunnel. Normally a golf cart was used to move around below, but John liked using his custom, four passenger Polaris. It had a hard shell winter enclosure, and eight speaker sound with a special navigation kit. Molly loved it.

John turned one of the linen closet's knobs to the left; it opened revealing the elevator; John and Molly got in, and pressed the lab button. When the elevator stopped and the door opened, Molly took off jumping into the cargo bed of the Polaris. John opened the driver side door then leaned over and opened the passenger side. In a second Molly was sitting up next to him, *we're going outside for sure.*

John drove straight for about eight hundred yards, passing several lab doors; now under the back of the property, past the shooting stations, until they came to the final station. He turned right onto a metal platform; hit a button on the visor and up they went. John backed off the platform on to a gravel road that led to back exit of the compound. He pressed another button on the visor and a gate opened sliding to the left; he passed through and turned left on the paved road.

He drove for about ten seconds, "lights on now." John looked at his navigation system (NAV) and said, "Coffee west of Jonesborough." He looked over; Molly was fully engaged.

As John followed the NAV his mind wondered back to the alarm situation. He had run diagnostics several times and it was working perfectly. He had checked the door and jams nothing to show tampering; besides it was almost impossible for anything except birds to get on the property.

Several weeks ago he had gone up to the widow's suite and had seen creatures moving around; he figured they were squirrels or other large rodents. As they moved about they seemed to dive into holes in the ground and disappear.

He had walked the property several times with Molly and she never acted like there was anything to get sniffed up about. He wondered if Sims had seen many animals up at the front house.

Sims was due at John's house at 7:00am for their daily ten on ten shooting contest. Sims was the group's firearms expert. He was teaching John to shoot like a sniper. "Turn right in three hundred feet," caught his attention. He looked hard and still almost missed the turn. As he drove on he found what looked like a small general store, gas station, diner, and The Coffee Hole.

Chapter Three

4:10 am

West of Jonesborough

John was wondering if The Coffee Hole was a spin-off of The Watering Hole, a common name for a local bar. As he got closer he could see several bulbs in the very old sign were not working. He pulled in, told Molly to stay, and got out. He looked closer. The original sign had read The Best Coffee and Donut Holes; now, as if by fate, it said, The Coffee Hole.

The Coffee Hole was as much of a donut shop cliché as it could be; right down to the red Formica counter and table tops. It was white on the inside with checker board, black and white linoleum floors and back in the day florescent light fixtures.

As he got to the door he could see three customers and an Asian man behind the counter. He went in. The coffee smelled good and he could tell fresh dough was frying in the back; so far pretty good.

Two of the customers sat across from each other, at a table even with the counter, on the left. The other customer sat at the counter just right of them; turned on his stool so he could be part of the conversation. The aisle to the back of the store and restrooms went between them.

John nodded to them and asked for a large coffee. What he got was twenty ounces of bliss. He found a table on the same aisle, but on the right side, third table back. He faced the street, his back to the others so he could watch Molly; he was wondering if he should let her out to pee.

John was half way through his coffee, thinking about a refill, when the guy sitting at the counter asked, "You trying to find your way to Knoxville? Need to find highway 81?" John, turned his chair towards him, "No I just told my NAV system to find me coffee west of Jonesborough and here I am."

The guy stood up and started toward John to join him. He was about five foot ten inches tall with black hair, bushy eyebrows, dark eyes; a lean, strong, wiry type; maybe thirty-eight years old. He was wearing black jeans with a red, black and white flannel shirt jacket. He spun a chair around and straddled it so he could lean on the back with his chest; he put his coffee down stuck out his hand,

"I'm Adam." John took his hand, "Good to meet ya Adam, I'm John Hart."

John had the feeling he was about to have his first encounter with the real natives of the area. Adam took a sip of his coffee, "You're not from 'round here are ya?" John enjoyed the slow Tennessee accent of the people he had met; he sat back in his chair letting the conversation come to him, "Well, I've been in this area about two years now, but just moved into new my house seven months ago."

Adam nodded, "What did you do the other seventeen months?" John smiled, "I oversaw the building of the place." Adam perked up, "So you're a home builder?" "No, I'm kinda in the cell phone business." Adam was now confused, "You live in Jonesborough and you are in the cell phone business? Doesn't seem there would be much of a market round here?" "Well, let's say it this way; I have manufacturing plants all over the country, and we're doing pretty well."

John got up, "Need a refill." He went to the counter; the Asian guy was in the back. John leaned over the counter a little, "Can I get a refill?" He could feel the two other customers looking at him; he nodded again. They grinned like they knew something he didn't.

The Asian guy came around the corner with flour all over his hands, and he seemed mad as hell, "What you want? I am very busy, what you want?" John stepped back a bit, "I would like a refill please." The Asian guy looked at John then at the other guys, "What, you the Emperor; you can't pick up the pot and pour coffee yourself?" John stepped in a little, gave the guy a look, "I can pour coffee; how much for the refill?" The Asian guy was about to speak when the biggest of the two others said, "Phu, go back to work and stop picking on this poor guy; he doesn't know the rules round here; refills are free."

The biggest guy was at least six foot six inches tall and two hundred and ninety pounds. He had blond hair, bright blue eyes, a weathered face and no neck. He seemed around forty years old. He was wearing bib-overalls with heavy work boots; he looked like he played in the NFL.

John turned to say something and bumped into Adam who was now right behind him. Adam stepped back, "These are my friends. This big guy is called Hoss he has a hay farm northwest of town" Hoss nodded. "This is my other buddy Joe, but everyone calls him Lil Joe. Joe was six foot tall and one hundred sixty-five pounds; same age as Adam. Joe had crew cut brown hair, brown eyes gaunt looking in the face; not really a little guy at all. He was dressed much the same as Adam, but his jacket was green white and black.

John was about to comment when he heard Phu behind him, "Day call him Lil Joe becuss he dick is whomungus." John spit up some of his coffee and just barely kept it from coming out his nose.

John thanked Phu for the refill, "So you are Vietnamese, import or domestic?" Phu looked at him strangely, "I come from the killing fields of Cambodia and by way of the boat people." Adam, intervened, "Bullshit he went to high school with us back in the day. He fakes the accent; he just doesn't like Chinese people; he is chink-a-phobic." John stuck out his hand, "Very honored to meet you Haing Ngor." (Google The Killing Fields movie). John smiled and went back and sat down facing their table. Phu, somewhat baffled, "Real wise ass we got here". Adam was back at the counter. John was really enjoying his coffee when it hit him; Hoss, Adam, Lil Joe and the Asian cook. They were either jerking his chain or he had stepped on to the Ponderosa and into an episode of Bonanza, (http://youtube.be/4EJebBY-YkO).

Now that they we're friends, Hoss asked, "John where exactly is this place you built?" John held up one finger, and went out to the car; he petted Molly as he turned on the NAV, hit reverse directions and got the spot. He came back in and was about to give Hoss the info when Phu, now speaking domestically, "You got your dog in the car? If it's got good manners, let it in." John said thanks and went back out and got Molly. She came in and laid at his feet. John continued, "The NAV says 5.6 miles east, southeast." Hoss was computing in his head, "Is it surrounded by tall thick, bushes that block all visibility?" "That's the one."

Hoss looked at Adam, "Adam and I went over there one day and tried like hell to see what was going on; lots of noise and dust, but couldn't see anything. You got something you don't want people to see?" All four of them were waiting to hear the big mystery, "Just me. I like my privacy; not much of that in California."

John changed the subject trying to deflect questions about the compound; saying he needed some advice about critters. How he can see them but can't make out what they are. They seem to run across the open area then dive into the ground. John told them he and Molly had checked for ground hog holes, or whatever, and found nothing.

They didn't bite. They wanted to know how much land and how much of it was forest and how much pasture. John didn't give up, "Hey, I think these things are setting off my alarms; I run diagnostics and the system is performing. When it goes off I hurry to check it out, but by the time I get to it, it has reset green."

They all looked at each other, then started to nod, Lil Joe said, "Raccoons." John, looking puzzled, "Raccoons?" Lil Joe looked John straight in the eye and continued, "Yup, they are sneaky little bastards, they will screw with you just for the fun of it." "Would they mess with the doors to your house?" Hoss jumped in, "Sure, those little assholes find ways to get past the locks, get into our barns, and tear the shit out of the place."

John was starting to feel maybe they were messing with him, so he pressed his luck, "OK then, what about the critters I see at dusk? They appear to be yellowish white, are faster than hell, and disappear into the ground?" Adam looked at Hoss, who was looking at Lil Joe and smiled. They all turned and looked squarely at John and with straight faces and said in unison, "Albino raccoons, they are the worst." They all burst out laughing. Molly got excited and moved from one to the other seeming to share in the joke.

John recovering, "Well, I guess I'll have to upgrade to video in those areas." Phu chimed in using an exaggerated Chinese accent, "They are cockey, rodent looking sonna bitches. They will give you the finger right there on TV. I once put my own piss round my garbage cans to keep them out. Next morning, I find they had shit all over my front porch. They are bad creatures."

John wanted to let them know that he was wise to them from the very beginning, still laughing he raised his cup, "Here's to the Ponderosa." As he brought his cup down he saw each one of them looking at him. Lil Joe said, "What is that; some kind of California toast? What does that even mean?" John kept looking at them then shook his head, "Nothing at all. I am just really enjoying being here right now." Phu shaking his head, "We love you to Gracie; howz that; boy we're havin' fun now?" They all laughed; John shut up and drank his coffee. Molly nudged his leg; he took her outside to pee.

Chapter Four

John and Molly were heading home via reverse NAV. He still wasn't sure about the Bonanza thing; he thought they had to be jerking his chain. He would think of a way to trip them up.

He was taken back a bit by his own attitude, *am I going back?* He thought it could be a good idea; like they were friends. He felt good right now; the depression that usually lasted five to six hours was gone. He smiled *better results than therapy.* Molly moved to the back seat and curled up.

He turned his attention to the alarm problem; he ran it all back through is mind; he needed to understand what was going on. He figured Sims was coming at 7:00am; together they could make a plan. He knew tonight's dream would be the worst of the three; he didn't want a repeat of last night.

He had to pay attention now; the NAV had no way of finding the back of the compound. He pulled into the lift, went down, backed out into the tunnel, and headed back to the house.

This time he parked under the kitchen and went up the dumb waiter, or service lift. Molly hoped it was breakfast time; she was right. Kibble for her and cereal for John. She always compared what they were eating, *both having kibble, all's fair.*

John's kibble was granola, Kat's favorite blend. She was in Prague doing research, sketching and painting; probably some shopping. Kat had been with John since before the settlement; she was there when the dreams started. She had short blond, wispy hair, was a petite five foot eight inches tall, with brownish green eyes. Kat was tough as dragon scales.

She died with him every month; but she was like Molly, very empathetic. It damaged her to see him go through the terror and hurt. She was a critical factor in his ongoing recovery; but she could only take so many dream cycles; then she had to have a break. She felt guilty at first, but John assured her it was imperative; and they worked it out. He thought of the Ming chamber pot; he forced tonight out of his mind.

While eating he thought of phone calls he had to make; bases needed to be touched. He would discuss the alarm with Glenn, but first a call to his brother Nick. Nick and John were foster brothers raised by the same mom; without a man in the house. Even though they were not related they were brothers.

Just as he picked up the phone, Molly put her head on his left thigh; time to go out front. John put down the phone. John fetched the ball from her toy bucket in the kitchen corner and headed to the front doors.

He went out and Molly slowly followed behind. It was not quite full light; just that almost can see, but not really, kind of dark. Molly went down the south steps and about fifteen feet out on the grass and did her business. John almost scolded her for not running out into the front, but thought better of it. Something was not right.

Molly returned and acted like she wanted back in the house. John went down the front steps and walked without looking back. He went a good thirty feet and turned around; Molly was still sitting by the front door. He called her; she looked left then right; then turned and put her right paw on the door handle. John didn't understand her behavior. He gave her a good head scratch then let her in; she ran back to the kitchen and laid under the table.

John made his calls; touching bases and learning about the installation of the alarm system from

Glenn. Glenn Berquist, was a lifelong friend of John's and was in charge of all things in the cyber world. He had acted as general contractor for the Jonesborough compound. The compound looked like a big fancy house, but was in fact a technological facility that rivaled any in the world.

Glenn had some disturbing news concerning a Chinese hacker name Zhang Jie. Zhang had been tearing up the computer industry; he hunted secrets. He was tied to several murders, technology theft, abductions to leverage secrets, and capture for transport. Three company leaders had been killed in, "accidents" that Glenn had traced back to Zhang and his men.

Glenn noticed lately Zhang had started looking at the cellular market. He was worried he would accidently find a thread into Gavin Tanner's company. John logged it all away for now, told Glenn to put together a threat assessment and get it to him. John signed off abruptly; something else was bugging him. Nick would have to wait.

He got the ball out of Molly's bucket and headed for the door. Molly was at the front doors way ahead of him. He paused at the door, "You ready to go?" Molly was spinning, she was ready to go. He opened the door, the sun was up, so he threw the ball as far as he could and she went after it.

He knew she wasn't afraid of the dark, or new people and places. She had attacked intruders when he was in California. She was afraid of something in the front…when it was dark. He felt a twinge go down his spine; this really bothered him, Molly was fearless. Then it hit him, *why hadn't she been barking before the alarms went off?*

Chapter Five

6:50am

Gun Shed,

Hart Compound

John was heading to the gun shed when he saw Sims arriving in his golf cart. He stared at Sims a moment having a flashback of how Sims had looked in his dream; no body, growling at him like an animal, "Ah, after we get done, if you got time, I want to get your input on a few things." Sims could tell John was bothered by something; he would cheer him up, "Well, it shouldn't take long to kick your ass on the range, then sure no problem. Molly?" "I don't want her down here too much, no doggie earplugs."

Sims had come to the group via Glenn. Sims had been Glenn's Sergeant in Afghanistan. They had gotten close working together to bring the cyber geek squad at Bah Gram Airbase to some semblance of physical fitness. At Six foot, one hundred seventy-eight pounds, with course, blond hair, kept short, and jade green eyes; Sims was a picture of intensity.

When Sims came home to the States, he found his wife and daughter had left him behind. He found Glenn and tried to start a new life.

John and Glenn put Sims back together. He had tried to kill himself with Jack Daniels and bar room brawls. He was trying to pay himself back for his family leaving him; somehow he thought it was his fault.

He and John hit it off right from the start. John hired Sims to get the group in shape and fighting ready. Sims took John from a physical mess to a pretty lethal machine. They would spar and shoot all the time. John needed to vent his anger. He could try to kill Sims for hours at a time and never really hurt him. Sims knew how much punishment it took to bring John out of his post dream funk.

Sims lived alone in the very nice four bedroom house at the main entrance of Hart's compound. His house was what most observers believed to be the main house. The mail, deliveries and the like went to Sims' house because it appeared to be the only house on the property. The house was set up like a bed and breakfast designed to house guests, and group members, for long periods of time.

Sims, like Glenn, had to wear several hats. He was in charge of the physical security and maintenance of the compound proper. He was responsible for every inch of the grounds except the main house and the shooting stations. Although he was in command of the gun shed. Sims took care of the group's security teams, their firearms and tactical training.

There were three out buildings on the property, a garage for the vehicles, the machine shop to facilitate repairs, and a maintenance shed was attached to the machine shop, which was filled with mowers and garden tools. There was also a stable and pens for farm animals of which they had none.

All of the out buildings were connected on the surface by a gravel road with a white picket fence boarding it. The buildings were connected underneath the surface by a large, well-lit tunnel system that went forth from Sims house. There was also a straight line tunnel from the back of Sims' house to the main house and gun shed.

The gun shed was in the back of the property and was shielded from view by a fence with the same large foliage which surrounded the entire compound. Beyond that there was an 800 yard shooting range with three shooting stations.

The gun shed was a two story building with a glass front and more of the foliage on the remaining three sides. There were two entrances from ground level and one from the tunnel. The first ground level entrance led to the main living area, or recreation room, the second had steps leading to the second floor barracks. There were steps in the rec-room that led to the roof and sniper's lair.

Sims and John entered the lower floor. Sims opened one of the side doors on the left that looked like where the restroom would be; he came out a moment later with three identical targets. The targets were silhouettes of a male's head; they were to scale. Sims went back toward his golf cart, "I'll get going on these you get the hardware. We are shooting the old dog .308 rifle with its standard issue Weaver scope from 1975." John turned and paused for a moment to figure the fastest way to get what they needed.

Behind the walls on all three sides were hallways filled with gun safes and cabinets full of ammunition, scopes and reloading equipment. John decided to go right to gather the small items; then around to the old Winchester .308. He was in luck the scope needed was already mounted.

When John stepped out on the deck with all the gear, he looked up at the closest shooting station and saw Sims putting up the first target. There were three stations, all identical, and all two hundred yards apart. From the deck to the first one was two hundred and so on out to eight hundred yards at the back fence.

Each station looked like a cinder block garage with a flat roof that had a sixty foot electrical tower on top. The last seventeen feet of the towers looked like a giant closed umbrellas ready to open and deflect the rain. The main access to the stations was from the tunnel below. The target adjustment cables ran at the forty foot level.

The umbrellas' surfaces were covered with receptors; some solar and some signal. When the umbrellas opened up, they became satellite dishes. Each dish could be used in conjunction with each of the other stations or ganged together as a single station. When all three stations and the roof of John's house worked together, it was NSA, eat your heart out.

It was weird to see Sims come down the ladder disappear into the station; and a minute later he would pop up at the next station. Each target was placed on a steel plate that moved along a cable system.

The remote allowed them to move the targets forward or back and get exact distances. Sims disappeared for the last time and John's cell phone rang, "250, 475, 685" Sims said and hung up; John moved the targets into position, loaded the clips with the rounds from 1973, and laid it all out for Master Sergeant Sims to inspect.

The rotation went like this: Both took their 685yrd shot first from the sniper nest. Second three shots from the second floor deck at 475yrds, and the next three from the lower level at 250ft. The final three shots were taken back in the Sniper's nest and the scores tallied. They had seven minutes to complete the course.

The first shooter would complete the course, and then the second shooter would follow. Even though John could easily qualify as a sharp shooter, he rarely beat Sims. John had missed his first shot by one inch and hit seven out of nine head shots. Sergeant Sims hit his first shot and eight out of nine head shots.

Sims cleaned up the targets and John put away the gear. John went into the bright white chef's kitchen; it had all stainless, professional grade appliances. He took a couple of beers out of the fridge. He sat at the kitchen table and looked into the recreation room.

There was lots of seating without space eating sectionals. There were two big screen TVs; one in the middle of the east wall and the other in the middle of the south wall.

You could play pinball and other games along the north wall. There were two couches that rolled out into beds and recliners that lay flat. There were sleeping bags and air mattresses in the closets.

Below there were enough supplies to hold out for months. Also, that is where the real weapons and survival equipment was. Above was a room filled with a dozen twin beds aligned in three rows. There were two bathrooms; each with a triple head shower layout.

Sims came in, set the targets down by John, and went to the kitchen sink to wash his hands. He cleaned up the area, dried his hands, and reached over John's shoulder and grabbed his beer.

Sims sat in one of two recliners that were facing down range. John dropped the targets in Sims' lap and flopped in the chair to the left, "A total of an inch and a half between a tie and loosing badly." "Same distance between being grazed on the forehead or on your way to hell my friend."

John let out a long sigh, "Sims, I need your help. There is some weird shit going on around here and I can't figure it out." Sims sat up in his recliner leaned over and looked at him, "Lay it on me."

Chapter Six

7:15 am

Colorado Rockies

Glenn's environment was perfect. He was high in the Colorado Rockies above all the noise of the cities. From this location he could fully utilize his listening and transmitting station.

He had designed and built this site, and four others like it; the same time he had put together John's compound in Jonesborough. It had been a crazy time, but now hunting was a lot easier. Of the five stations this was his favorite.

He would work from all five of the sites throughout the year so no one could zero in on him. The best part of the entire system was that he could combine any of the five with the power of the main station at the compound in Jonesborough.

Glenn was protective by nature. He was always listening for those who could potentially do John or the group harm. His loyalty was absolute; he and John went way back; all the way back. It was always

John, his brother Nick and Glenn. Glenn was different in the fact he had a great home and support. Kat came along when John was in his last year of high school. John was the idea guy; Nick was smooth; a charmer, and Glenn took care of everything else.

Glenn was six foot three inches of long, strong, and crazy. His long brown hair and beard gave him a biker look, but his walk screamed stoner. His close friends sometimes called him Sasquatch.

He was pretty easy going, considering he was two hundred and fifteen pounds and known for taking care of business. He and John got along because they both had a sharp wit and liked to prank their friends. He was a delightful and fun loving human being; until he wasn't; and right now he wasn't.

He had called John earlier, but something was off. John seemed preoccupied with something else. When he blew him off about Zhang Jie's recent activity he knew.

When John was in dream mode he was somewhat distracted; it wasn't fun for any of them, especially him. Normally John would fight through those times; he would have jumped right on the Zhang Jie thing; instead he wanted a threat assessment. He needed John's full attention on this right now. Zhang Jie was pissing him off.

Zhang had a system. He would follow the big money in specific sectors of business. He would start with the major innovators, creators of the latest technologies and high ranking businessman in the largest companies.

Zhang would exploit weaknesses in them, their families or businesses. If he found information he would steal it. He was a master at finding those individuals that Chinese Intelligence could manipulate, intimidate or kidnap to procure what information they wanted.

Glenn had seen what he had done to the computer industry the last four years; now Zhang Jie had turned his gaze to cellular technology, and communications.

Glenn was an exceptional hunter, highly skilled and stealthy. Glenn's greatest asset was the fact he had no reputation in the cyber world. No one knew who he was. He had never held a related job, didn't attend a big school and his military service was a boring as it could get. In all his hunting no one he had tracked had even felt he was there, let alone catch him.

He had picked up Zhang as he entered the U.S. to attend UCLA, in California. Zhang had no idea Glenn had been observing him for the past five years.

In the five years of studying Zhang, Glenn now knew he was a very dark and sadistic person. Searches of his browsers revealed many disturbing websites that he frequented. He was fascinated by young American girls; and not in a good way.

Now Glenn worried that Zhang would be drawn to John's flagship operation in Knoxville, Tennessee. Confidante was the only cell phone maker of its kind. First, they manufactured in the United States. Secondly, they made high end burner phones. The phrase, "High end burner phone", was an oxymoron; that was their hook.

People who were in the Net Jets crowd needed phones that were sexy, could perform, and be disposable. John had seen to it; these were loaded with all the latest features that the cell industry had to offer. He sold them at one fourth the cost of the high end makers. At a hundred and fifty dollars, "The Confidant" was a steal.

Of course these phones were not hanging on the walls in Wal-Mart. The Confidant required a subscription. Certain companies that catered to the rich and mobile offered them to their clients in their gift bags; free stuff. The client could then renew their usage directly from Confidante. Confidante also mass produced quality burners for a wide range of customers and sold them worldwide.

Confidante's products were actually a cover for the facility itself. It was the lab where John proto-typed all of the group's inventions. The plant was divided into floors. The top floor was where the everyday business was carried out.

The lower levels housed the remaining three working floors, where the classified research and development took place. They were monitored by the Pentagon. They required very stringent security provisions. One of the security protocols required deployment of specialized military units that would be able to protect the facility in cases of attack or breach. They were referred to as Mil Spec Units. Confidante had a group of twenty specialists that secured the lower levels.

Confidante was a privately held company and was extremely profitable. John needed to avoid the market hype that came with success and the stock exchange. John's mantra, "Cool and quiet is how we go; avoid causing ripples in the water."

Glenn knew once Zhang had started looking at Confidante, he would be looking into Gavin Tanner its' President and Owner. If Zhang found any record of Confidante's classified status there would be trouble. Zhang Jei knew that kind of security meant new technology. John was very invested in Gavin. He was the first of John's projects.

Chapter Seven

8:45am,

Gun Shed Rec-Room

John was trying to work out a sequence of events for Sims, "I guess it was about three or four weeks ago around 7:00pm, I took some beers up to the widow's suite to relax and survey what we've accomplished here thus far." Sims nodded with raised eyebrows, "This place is amazing."

John turned his eyes to the ceiling, "The sun had just set and I thought I saw animals moving across the front grass area; about half way to your house. I thought how did they get passed the fencing already, maybe they could be ground hogs or something. I did that two nights in a row; there were more creatures on the second night.

"Whatever these things are, they seem very strange. They are a light yellowish color, like a lemonade deal; they are quick and can disappear into the ground in a flash. So I am thinking maybe these things could be setting off the alarms.

"I went out with Molly in the morning to look for scat or ground hog holes; we saw nothing. We have walked this property several times and she has never sniffed out anything.

I have regularly checked the doors for marks or damage; nothing. All the alarm's diagnostics on the system says it doing its job. I verified it all with Glenn; he says there should be no problems."

Sims was rocking in his recliner looking at John with a half-smile on his face. John widened his eyes, "Well?" "Oh shit, you were serious? You lost me at lemonade." "Yes! I've got to figure this out. Molly won't even go out the front at night now. The alarms trips show only on the south side kitchen entry.

"Last night, at 1:00am, I was trying recover from one of my dreams, and the fucking alarm goes off, boom! I am on my ass. I try to see what was going on and I passed out; Molly woke me up at 2:50am and the alarm had reset."

John up and pacing, "I need you to help me find out what is scaring the shit out Molly, and what the hell is tripping the alarms.

"The guys at the Coffee Hole are telling me its raccoons." Sims still rocking; he put on his serious face, "The Coffee Hole?" John lost it, raising his voice, "Damn it Sims this isn't funny. Have you seen anything? Seen any animals around while you're working?" "No I haven't seen any lemonade creatures, but from the front of my house I have seen some squirrels and a few ground hogs. We're not counting birds, right?" John stood up took Sims' beer and threw it in the trash, "Thanks for the help friend." "Ok, ok let's talk this out."

Sims got up and sat at the kitchen table, "Did you see them off and on at night when you took Molly out the front?" "No, but this morning she wouldn't go out front; she stayed close to the house, then back in as fast she could. I tried to make her follow me out front, but she was havin' none of it."

Sims thinking, "So it is safe to say that you are not in a hurry to get to sleep tonight. So let's go back up to the widow's suite and have a few beers, but this time we take a couple of night scopes with us."

Sims went to the fridge and got another beer, "We can chart what we see; maybe shoot one to see if lemonade comes out." John just shook his head, "You gonna be good company or do I have to kick your ass." Sims smiled and whispered, "You've been getting close boss, but you're not ready for prime time. I will behave." John sat down near Sims, "I will get the stuff and put it in the suite, say 6:00pm. We can watch the stages of light to see if that is the determining factor as to when these guys come out; if at all."

Sims stood and stretched, "Do you have a security panel in the suite as well?" "Yup full panel in every room with the small panels the bathrooms." Sims grabbed the targets, "I will record these. Is Molly gonna be there?" "Yup" "Good someone to talk to; see ya at 6pm. Oh, I can make some food or should we eat first?" John thought a second, "Eat first, Molly's gotta eat round 5pm at the latest. You could bring the Beer Nuts." Sims spun around, "Beer Nuts? What are you a hundred years old? I'll get something; Beer Nuts? God help us."

It was 9:30am and he had to let Molly out; he had been way too long. He walked back to house, climbed the steps up to the back deck, went through the French doors, and right into the kitchen. He looked around, "Hey doggie where you at?" He heard Molly's nails on the floor. He moved quickly and opened the back doors. She blew through them, down the deck, on back lawn, head down looking for a good spot

Chapter Eight

John owed Glenn an explanation for his behavior earlier. He should call him right away. He was unsettled by what Glenn had found; his tone was serious, and he didn't like the sound of it. John needed information right away; he hoped Glenn could steer this Zhang Jie asshole in another direction.

He felt that the NSA knew about this guy but wouldn't move on him. They would wait until they needed something from China. God forbid they protect those who drove the economy that paid for all their toys. John thought, *that's why we take care of our own; we can't let him find Gavin.* He took out his phone and set the encryption and called Glenn.

Gavin Tanner was now an urban legend in the cellular industry; John's first project had paid off big time. Gavin came to the group three years ago, after John, Nick and Glenn had completed the Confidante plant, and were in their second year of production. Nick, Jess Williams and Sims had been the managers running the day to day operations, now John needed them back doing their own jobs within the group. It was time to find an owner.

Glenn had come across Tanner on one of his evaluations of the cellular market place. Gavin was one of four successful Vice Presidents of Engineering within a huge cellular phone company. He was doing great work.

Tanner was forty-one years old, was married six years, without children thus far. He was five foot eleven inches tall, with thick salt and pepper hair, more pepper then salt, extremely well groomed with blue eyes. He looked like he was a little strong and a little athletic; Sergeant Sims made sure that little bit went a long way.

Tanner had a vision for where the cellular market should go. He had pushed for more research into the power side of the tech. More juice, more range, and a phone that would never have to be recharged. His CEO and colleagues told him to slow down. They wanted to extract every penny they could get from their gadget obsessed customers.

Nick was the one who approached Gavin the first time. He had one of his security men learn his haunts and habits. On Thursdays, at lunch, Gavin Tanner went to look at cars he couldn't afford.

On a beautiful Thursday afternoon in 201, in Basking Ridge, NJ, Nick Hart parked himself in the customer's waiting area of the dealership Gavin visited during his lunch time. There was free coffee, it was very private, and it was the only way in; only way out.

Nick was medium height, and build, and he was very strong for his weight. Sims had turned him into a very quick hitting, maximum damage kick boxer. He had jet black hair, almost black eyes; he looked and acted like a fixer.

He was gifted in the way he talked to people; they naturally seemed to trust him. He was honest, direct and could cut you with his wit if need be. Nick was a good man; he had taken care of John all the years he couldn't take care of himself.

Nick smiled when Tanner came through the door, "Here to pick up your car?" Gavin stopped and looked at Nick who was dressed like someone who could own the dealership, "Oh no. I just come here at lunch to drool. I could never justify one of these."

Nick stood up, took a couple of steps towards Gavin, and put his hands in his pockets, "What if you could?" Gavin let his head lean to the right, sizing up Nick, "What are you trying to say?" "I am saying I would like to discuss your future with you. I

48

have a client who is very interested in talking to you?" Now Tanner put his hands in his pockets, "You mean a job offer? I already have a job Mister….?" "Hart, Nick Hart. I am a match maker so to speak." "A headhunter you mean, you get twenty percent when you place someone, yes?" Nick moved closer, looked left then right, "I only have one client, and I do really well, thank you…twenty percent, really? Geeeez."

Nick motioned to the seating area and said, "You got twenty minutes until they will miss you. How about I tell you what we see you doing for the next fifteen years?" Tanner smiled and started to move towards the chairs, "I'll bite." Nick pulled his hands out of his pockets, moved beside Gavin, put his hand on Tanner's elbow and leaned in close, "We have a company we want you to own." Tanner stepped back, a skeptical look on his face, "Are you the Nigerian Prince that wants to give me five million dollars?" Nick looked left again then right again and smiled, "Five million, really? Geeeez."

Gavin started to look a little pissed off. Nick raised his hands and said, "I am not kidding. We have been watching you. We have been waiting for you to leave your present situation, but you haven't done so. We know you are frustrated with the lack of vision there.

"You have given them ample time and reason to change course. Your vision is currently being wasted. We want you to join us. We have been steadily preparing to implement your, or our, vision.

"Mr. Tanner, we would like to pay you a hundred thousand dollar consulting fee to sit down with us for one week. Let us tell you our plan. Let us try to convince you that you are the perfect man to blow this industry up. If the money is not the way you want to go, let us lease any car at this dealership for you for the next year. If you decide to join us it is yours. If you don't, then we will cover the lease return and all expenses."

Nick leaned back and crossed his legs, "We know you have three weeks' vacation due to you. We hoped a working vacation with your wife would be a great idea.

"We want your wife with you for the final round of our negotiations. If you decide to take our offer you will have a lot of changes to deal with. She will have to fully understand what is happening and understand how this will change your lives. "My estimation is that you will have to decide how you can possibly live on nine million dollars a year. Oh, and that task will get harder each year we perform."

Nick uncrossed his legs, leaned forward again, "Would you like me to take you to the bank? Should

I hail the sales manager? Maybe you could call work and tell them some things came up. We could go get something to eat and I could answer some of your questions. You have five minutes to call or run back to work?"

Nick didn't like the fact that Tanner sat there with his eyes boring into his, and then he reached for his phone. When the call connected, "Yes, this Gavin Tanner, I have a family emergency I have to deal with. I am OK yes, and I won't be back until Monday." He put away his phone. Standing up he looked Nick in the eyes, "First, I am starving. Second, I have a whole lot of questions, and finally, I hope you have packed for the weekend." Nick stood, reached out and shook Gavin's hand, "This is going to be a really fun weekend."

Chapter Nine

This was the time of the day that was the worst. The day would drag on and on. He didn't want night to come, but he needed the day to end. He went into the kitchen got himself an energy drink, trying not to wake Molly. She was sacked out in her doggy bed next to her bucket of toys; of course her ball was right at the end of her nose as she slept.

He had talked to Glenn and it appeared they would have some time to prepare for Zhang Jie. They discussed several options that might buy them more time, but it was obvious they were going to need help.

Now that he had some solid information he could start taking action. Nick would have to arrange a sit down with General Jack Rouse. Rouse would have to check his sources at the NSA.

John would send Sims to Confidante to talk with Tanner's security people. For all John knew there may be people watching them already; Glenn didn't think so, but agreed it was possible he had not found everyone who had bad intentions. Sims and Glenn would work out the logistics for an end game if they ended up on their own.

John wanted to talk with General Rouse himself and let him know that Nick was on the way. He wanted to discuss how they could keep an even lower profile at Confidante.

He was hoping that he could change the way his people were housed in the area; currently it screamed government employees. Rouse would have to go to the facility in civilian dress or not go at all. People with government cars should be given cars that are not standard Army issue. These were all points they had argued before; before there was a Confidante; back when there were extreme trust issues between John and Jack Rouse; back in 2009.

To put it mildly John did not go through normal channels to get the military to embrace the group's new technologies. General Jack Rouse had been targeted by John and Nick to help market their products. They intentionally placed him in the center of an extremely touchy situation.

Their hacking of the Pentagon led to Confidante, it led to the advancement of multiple military weapon systems and covert surveillance. This one event cemented a great relationship between General Jack Rouse, the US Military and John's group. One day that literally changed the world.

In February 2009 General Jack Rouse was seated in the back of his rank specific vehicle, with his assigned driver; well on his way to the Epic Smokehouse. He did so every Thursday afternoon at 4:00pm. It was in Pentagon City; just a swing around North Rotary Road, right on South Fern Street, across Army Navy Drive, passed the Residence Inn; seven hundred feet on the left. In less than six minutes he was face first in Knob Creek.

John and Nick were standing on the corner of South Fern and Army Navy as the General drove by; John noted the time and Nick noted the speed. They had been staying at the Residence Inn on and off for the last three weeks; they always made it back for Thursdays at the Epic Smokehouse. Nick said, "They entered the intersection at thirty miles per hour. Because of the drainage dip across the road, they slowed to three miles per hour to avoid bottoming out. They started gaining speed after the ass end of the car cleared the dip." John smiled, "They are consistent. The variability' in our measurements isn't even worth calculating. The time of arrival at the intersection from our first visual is within seconds; speed in out of the dip, within three percent.

John Hart had several things to consider; arrival time, speed through the intersection, what distance Nick had to be from the curb, and how fast he had to walk into the street. Nick had to time it so the general's car would stop just as it hit him.

The last point was where John would be standing as it all unfolded. He felt he should be on the other side of the street. He had to be close enough to clone the General's phone with the car doors shut; with a door open it was a piece of cake even at thirty yards. There was a good chance he would get info from both the phones in the vehicle. They could deal with all that after the job was done.

Nick would be dressed for success, pulling his rolling suitcase, and engaged in a life and death phone call. After contact with the car he would scramble to his feet. While he was yelling and screaming he would hit send on his phone; and place the decoding software on their phones; doors not an issue. If by chance the car did not hit him, Nick would do his best New York pedestrian, "I'm walkin' here! I'm walkin' here!"

They went back to their room at the Residence Inn. They noted the front door of the Hotel was a hundred-ten feet from the middle of the intersection facing west; people exiting the Hotel were naturally facing the intersection. No doubt someone would see the General smack into Nick.

Once inside their room they gathered up their prototype cell phones and took a walk. They were relaxed; they had another thirteen days before they would get the information they needed.

They walked west on Army Navy to South Joyce street and turned left. They wanted to eat at Saigon Saigon; they were craving noodle soups.

They found a table that afforded a view of the main eating area. They were happy to see that General Rouse's driver needed soup as well. It was hot tea for him; hold the Knob Creek. Nick took out his phone and set it on the table so the business end was aimed at the driver. Since it looked like any other cell phone, he was not worried about appearances. He reached over acting like he was responding to a text he hit boost mode and clone; within seconds the phone was fifty percent of the way done, then it was done.

John picked up his menu, "Why do that now?" "We can use it to exclude info quickly to I.D. the General's phone after the data grab." John waved at their server, "Excellent Pinky. Next month we take over the world." Nick looked at his phone, then put it back on the table.

They enjoyed their soup and continued their walk on South Joyce heading passed the River House Apartments; home of one General Rouse. They arrived at the Epic Smokehouse fourteen minutes later, concluding their seven tenths of a mile walk.

The General was seated at the last table far right as you could get. He sat facing the bar his back to the street. He was white haired now, just six feet tall and two hundred-ten pounds. In his day he was an inch taller, dark brown hair and twenty-five pounds lighter. He was a grunt in Viet Nam and was now overseeing several top secret projects. These projects varied from new weapons to advancements in communications and targeting.

General Jack was a no bullshit soldier. He figured that he could get in a few drinks, have a great meal and be home at the River House before the dinner crowd arrived. He was always discreet, as was the way of pentagon employees. "Cool and quiet as we go; avoid causing ripples in the water."

John and Nick sat at the first table on the right side, ten tables north of General Jack. They ordered drinks and a bread basket; soup would not be enough to soak up their Jack Daniels. Straight on ice and twist of lemon was how they both took it. When the bread came Nick asked their server if she would take the general another round of what he was drinking on them as a way to thank him for his service.

When she brought the General his drink, John saw the server point to them. General Jack looked up and raised his current drink and said, "Thank you boys, but can't receive a gratuity from anyone at any time, I appreciate it though."

The server left leaving the drink on the General's table. John stood up, "Ok, may I at least shake your hand sir?" Jack stood up, "It would be an honor." John and Nick walked to the General and shook his hand and thanked him again.

As John and Nick were turning to go the General was sitting down, "You boys work in Pentagon City?" John glanced at Nick, "No we are just here trying to figure some things out." "Like what?" Jack asked. John and Nick made a point to look at each other very nervously. John nodded and Nick started, "Ah, well that's the deal, we have something we need to talk to someone about, but we don't know who or how. We didn't think we should show it to anyone but the military, so we came down here. No plan just trying to do that."

General Jack was now on high alert. Was he being played? "You guys know who I am?" John looked at his collar insignias and said, "A General?" "Yes, nice guess, but do you know anything about me?" John looked confused and went into his Sherlock Holms routine, "You are a General, you like barbeque, and bourbon, and being alone in this place…but no we know nothing really." "You got any clue where I might work son?" Nick stepped in, "At the Pentagon?" Jack stared at them like, *Come on boys put it together.*" "Oh! We shouldn't be talking to you at all. We are so sorry." Nick turned to John, "Let's go he can't talk to us."

General Jack Rouse sat back down and drank his free drink in one pull. He was thinking hard about public meetings and protocols. He didn't think much of the two kids, but maybe that was their deal. In the end he settled on," *they wanted to thank me and I said too much";* so the Knob Creek took the brunt of the blame.

Chapter Ten

February 2009

Pentagon City

Two weeks later, like clockwork General Jack did what General Jack does; Nick Hart played his part of pissed off business man to perfection. John and Nick put the prototypes through their paces. All went well and General Jack never recognized either of them.

While going through the data captured in the phones, John had praised the mind numbing properties of bourbon. When they isolated the General's phone number and make of phone they were ready to execute their plan.

John had Nick call their lawyer to join them tomorrow. They got him a room and arranged for him to be brought to them after he landed. Going through the legal dance was going to be the difference between going to jail and getting paid twice.

Their lawyer was former General Jackson Dunn. He was with the same firm that represented John in his lawsuit against California Education. He was six foot three inches, black, very fit, age fifty-six, and a former leader of the Judge Advocate Generals or The Judge Advocate General; he had been the TJAG.

The appointment of TJAG was the end all; top of the heap. When he finished his four year term he retired to the private sector. He was more than qualified to deal with cases involving the military verses civil law.

Dunn was there to add his weight to the John's claims. They would realize that a former TJAG would not cross the line and represent criminals. He was there to explain all of John's contingencies.

If Dunn was asked why his firm would be involved with John, he would answer a fourteen million dollar retainer gets you the best.

Dunn got there the next morning; they had breakfast while going over the pitfalls of what lay ahead. If the general recognized them from the data grab they were toast. They could negotiate prison for the prototypes if they had to.

They wanted a settlement from a law suit for wrongful incarceration, and then sell them the technology; a long term development contract as the golden goose.

When they called General Rouse in his office at the Pentagon all hell was going to break loose. One, no one calls into the Pentagon without going through the security software and communications hub. Two, using experimental signals and decoding software inside the building without the government's knowing could be considered espionage. Three, General Rouse was going to be extremely pissed being at the middle of this whole thing.

General Rouse was going to lose his mind when Dunn tells his boss that Rouse had a chance to deal with the two perpetrators directly; he could have controlled the situation.

The trickiest part of the whole plan depended on the General answering his own phone; if the call was disconnected the decoding capability was gone, no chance for a second call. The decoding app translates the analog, 30 MHz signal to standard digital communication.

The low frequency selected is the same frequency elephants use to communicate. The boost mode powers the low, 30 MHz, signal the distance and rate needed for up to 25 minutes. The assumption is that no one is looking for communications at such low levels.

The best part was that anyone trying to find the offending signal would only look for digital signals because the General would be talking on a digital device.

It was Thursday, March 5th 2009; at 2pm John planned to make the call. Twenty minutes before the call they were all in position. John was alone in their room; he put in his ear piece and did a com check. Nick would monitor the call from the other side of the Residence Inn, to prevent them both from being arrested, and to save one of the prototypes.

Jackson Dunn would walk into the main entrance of the Pentagon at exactly 2pm. All the coms were working; time to go.

At exactly 2pm John pressed send and held his breath; there was a partial ring, then a full ring, then another, and finally, "You are go for General Jack Rouse." John almost peed himself, but pulled it together, "General Rouse this is one of the guys you talked to at the Epic Smokehouse three weeks ago. We told you we had something we wanted to share only with the military?" No response.

John could hear the Rouse snapping his fingers together, then the sound of paper being rustled about, "Yes, I remember. What was your name again?" "Oh, we didn't get that far, but I knew who you were because of your nameplate." "Yes, so are you going to introduce yourself?" John was almost jumping up and down now, "Well, I think I just did. You should be hearing soon from the switchboard that there is no call that came through them and it appears that you have your phone on but are not engaged in a call. I'll wait a minute until you catch up."

John checked the time remaining on his boost settings; now at twenty-four minutes.

General Rouse was silent for about ten more seconds and came back, "Well, you were correct we show nothing; pretty neat trick. Is this what you wanted to show the military?" John was really into it now; this was working and he had to bring it home, "Yes, don't you think we made the right decision? Wouldn't you like to see Putin's face if we surprised him like this someday? You know, just to say what's up."

The General still moving around, "Yup, that would be fun, but I take it there is a lot more involved than just hitting send." Then more sternly, "You know you just hacked the Pentagon?"

John's ass puckered a bit on hearing that, "No, I just called a friend to tell him I figured a way to talk to the military about our project. We would like to develop the full potential of the technology and be a contractor for Uncle Sam. This could be our job interview leading to a spec and bid. Still no luck on the trace?"

General Rouse was now taking this whole thing very seriously. He had half of the pentagon looking for something they had no idea how to find. One of the technicians actually took the phone from Jack and put to his ear, to verify that General Jack wasn't off the reservation.

Finally General Rouse's commanding officer came in the office and held up his hand, "Take a second." Nick taking into John's other ear, "Look out John here comes the big boys; be respectful now."

General Rouse told John to hang on a second his boss just came in. John heard mumbling and whispers then, "John, I just got a green light from the boss; what would take to get you in here?" John was quiet for a second, held the phone away, "Dunn, here we go; you're up." Dunn took the com from his ear and swallowed it; waiting for his part to begin.

John came back to the General, "Well, I have sent my lawyer to the main entrance so you can work with him on keeping me out of jail. He has been waiting since this call began. He can show you our plans for the law suit if you do arrest me.

When you get that all sorted out we can meet at the Epic Smokehouse for some dinner and Knob Creek; sound good? By the way, we know you are going to try and take this technology under the guise of national security and we kinda hope you do; that way we get paid twice and we will still be your contractors. My lawyer will show you that too." John heard Nick in his ear, "Ten minutes." He checked the boost; it showed nine.

The General's end was quiet for several seconds, "It's a date see you at the Smokehouse say in an hour?" John didn't take the bait, "If you are serious, it will take well into the night to cover all our lawyer has to show you...so I guess at this point you are not quite there. When you are finished with Mr. Dunn he will contact me; then he will set our dinner date. I think we're finished now; it's been nice." John disconnected.

In less than three minutes, Nick came back to their room with his bags packed, "Nice job John. I am proud of ya. No matter what, we have this forever. This shit was fun." Nick took John's phone, put it with the other prototype in his carry-on and headed towards the door, "John don't hang around here, get gone." Nick headed for his flight.

John took a few minutes to get back on track, but couldn't get the smile off his face. He was living now and he really liked his new brain. He packed up, went and closed out the two rooms. It was only 3pm; he had plenty of time to get out of town.

Jackson Dunn was waiting patiently with a somewhat weird smile and a contemplative look on his face. He was working out the location of the com he had swallowed. Using a rate of digestion verses the time since he ate it type of math deal, he figured that it could theoretically be in his lower intestine by the time they came for him. Dunn was smiling at the thought that if John contacted him in the middle of questioning, they would think he was literally talking out his ass. They came at 4:10pm.

He figured they had run him through facial recognition and knew more about him than his wife. The Master Sergeant took him to a conference room that was three rings in; the C ring he thought. He waited there another twenty minutes. Dunn knew the drill. He was surprised they were playing it this way; if they read his service record they knew Dunn was a big hitter, a no bullshit soldier.

When somebody did show he was surprised to be talking to JAG lawyer, one Lauren Day. Day shook Dunn's hand, "It is an honor to meet you Sir; you had quite a career." Dunn nodded, "Thank you, it keeps retirement in perspective." They exchanged cards then Lauren said, "Ok sir, what are your goals for this meeting?"

Dunn went through all of the situations that he and John had discussed; Lauren Day took no notes and didn't lose focus once. Dunn summarizing, "Look, my client just wants to help his country. Most entrepreneurs would sell their tech to the highest bidder without any consideration for the consequences of their actions. He is not in it for the money; he is very wealthy and has financed the project on his own dime." Then Dunn asked, "What are the goals of your client?"

Lauren Day stood, "Someone will be with you in a minute, shook Dunn's hand and left. The Master Sergeant returned, "Sir, we are not going to hold you at this time, but would like you to return tomorrow morning at 8:30am. Dunn gave the Sergeant his best TJAG look as to say, *hold me; really?* "Will you do that Mr. Dunn?" Dunn replied in the affirmative, and then followed the Sergeant to the main entrance.

Once in his car, he took a swing around North Rotary, right on South Fern Street, across Army Navy Drive passed the Residence Inn, seven hundred feet on the left to the Epic Smokehouse. In just six minutes he was face first in three fingers of

Rebel Yell, the Deep South's finest bourbon. His stomach growled; smiling, *not now John; not now.* The server came for his dinner order, "Someone is joining me for dinner; it will be a minute."

Chapter Eleven

February 2009

The Pentagon

When Jackson Dunn arrived right at 8:30 the next morning he was met at the door and taken back to the C ring, and a much larger conference room. He waited as before; at 9:00am the room began to fill up. There were plenty of big wigs in charge of big deals and what looked like an army of technicians.

Dunn made eye contact with every one of them checking to see if they knew who he was; they all did. This was the most fun Dunn had had since he retired.

When they got started General Rouse was curious about Dunn's relationship with his clients and how long it took to set up, "the sting." Dunn took it straight to General Rouse, "First, there was no sting; nothing planned. Three weeks previous to the call, at the Epic Smokehouse, you were asked by my clients the best way to tell the military about something it needed to know. You, General Rouse had it within your power, at that moment, to give them some advice; you chose to run them off.

"They wanted to thank you for your service; they did. You initiated small talk; asked them if they worked in Pentagon City. They said no, we are just here trying to figure some things out. You asked, like what. Then they told you and you cut them off; do you have another version for us General Rouse?" The General was about to lose his temper when he noticed everyone in the room was staring at him like he was the bad guy.

The General regained his composure, "I felt I had stepped into a possible scam for information; I never should have engaged them in conversation beyond a simple thank you." Dunn continued, "Did you have your phone with you sir?" Rouse replied, "Of course not, it was stowed in the car."

Dunn had turned the tables and was now running the interview, "Then there was no way for them to get your number; correct?" Rouse cocked his head to the left, "No, that is correct,"

Lauren Day, saved the General's ass by asking, "Mr. Dunn you went through several hours of prep with our caller; did you not think what he was planning was wrong?" "Ms. Day there was no prep. I was asked how to legally prevent the United States

Military from seizing their inventions and all their research.

I advised on suing for wrongfully seized goods or property and false arrest. I then researched those issues and then met with my mentor and advisor, Benjamin Creps as to the validity of my arguments." Day was now staring at Dunn with her mouth hanging open, "You and the TJAG that served previous to you, worked out the arguments you presented to me yesterday?" "Yes Mam."

It was quiet for a long time; big wigs whispering about it to one another until Brigadier General Banks leaned toward Dunn, "General Dunn why would you go to all of that trouble?" Dunn let out a long sigh, "With all due respect, finally someone asked the right question."

Dunn spent the next 15 minutes taking them through the abuse John had to endure; he told them about the trial and the settlement. Finally Dunn said, "Throughout the three years of the trial we saw John transform into an intelligent and caring human being. We were not simply his lawyers we became his family advocate in every sense of the word. John Hart is not what you're thinking he is. He just thought, "Hey why not just call the guy like any other businessman would?"

Dunn added, "Just a personal observation; if this technology gets in the wrong hands it would be a shit storm. Thank him and work with him and his people. You have a lot to gain. Arrest him and you will pay him twice; Creps is certain of it."

They all looked around then General Banks stood, "General Dunn, we will ask you to wait in the outer lobby while we process this; Master Sergeant escort General Dunn and get him something to drink."

Banks sat back down, "General Rouse?" Rouse shifted in his seat, "May we all speak freely?" "I think that would be best." Rouse stood and walked to the west wall and leaned against it, "Shit Sir, Creps and Dunn? There is a million to one chance that one of them might be part of a scam, but there is zero probability that both would be working for profit.

General Jack continued, "I think this is their way of making sure the Army has this tech first. How else do you avoid a full all branches bid on this? We step into it during an investigation and it is awarded to us; pretty slick." Banks agreed, "I don't think Dunn would ever mention Creps if that was not the case."

General Rouse turned to Banks, "Can we get Creps to represent us in the demonstration and contract negotiations?" "Smart, let them continue working together on our behalf.

"Ms. Day can you negotiate the initial meeting and all the paper work and protections for all concerned?" Day stood, "Yes sir, in my interview of General Dunn we discussed what those might be. He is at the Residence Inn; I will approach him. Will I be confirming that John Hart and friends will not be charged with a crime?" Rouse smiled, "I will arrest them if they don't show up for the meeting; tell him, "No law suit; paid just once.""

Chapter Twelve

John went into the kitchen and got a twelve pack of beer out of the beverage fridge. Molly always had to stick her nose inside and look at every shelf. Then she would sit and stare at the bottom shelf. She knew the small green bottles of sparkling water were hers.

She usually got one after she had worked hard chasing her ball. She could still hope; nothing ventured, nothing gained. John took two out and put them in the canvas bag. He couldn't remember what was in the fridge in the widow's suite so he threw in some snacks and headed up to the third floor.

The widow's suite was set directly above the dream room. So from the front, the house's character was determined by a very large peaked, 18ft wide dormer centered in an expansive roof; whose roof ridge ended in the center, at the base of the widow's suite. The widow's suite was a ten foot by ten foot square room with its roof pitched to match the dormer and all the other roof gables.

The suite had the same two over two windows that were below in the dream room. The windows started at three feet off the deck and carried to the roof. There were four of them on each side to give a 360 degree view. The entire house was beautifully pitched and angled with complete symmetry.

The suite was surrounded by a very old wood deck with railings done in the style of shore lined houses in Maine. This style was called a widow's walk; women would pace staring into the night; praying their loved ones home from sea; thus called The Widow's Suite.

John and Molly went up the stairway on the rear deck, and entered through to the rear door of the suite. Molly didn't get up there very often and was sniffing every nook and cranny. Once she was sure only the good guys had been there, she stuck her nose in the canvas bag.

John put away the rest of the night's provisions and poured a drink for Molly. She loved the sparkling water. It tingled on her tongue, and tickled her nose. She would take a lick, jump back and bark, then attack the water again. She would eventually finish the water and look at John proud of her victory;

while her tongue licked her nose as to abate the
tickle.

John knew he would have to take her out to pee
soon; this water went right through her. When that
time came, he would put her to bed in the kitchen
until he headed to the dream room for the night.

John looked at his watch and realized he was a bit
behind. He and Molly went down the stairs and kept
going across the back deck, down the steps, across
the cement deck, across the grass and to the gravel
road that led to the gun shed.

John saw Sims' golf cart and dropped his head; he
knew Sims would give him shit for not having the
suite filled with their toys already. John entered the
rec-room and saw all of the doors open; several
items had been thrown on the couch.

Sims came out of a door on the south, and was
greeted immediately by Molly. He gave her a good
scratch, "Come on little girl." She followed him into
the kitchen. She knew what was up, *the back-up ball!*
Sims retrieved it from the pantry and showed it to
her, walked to the entry door, and out on the deck.
He chucked it as far as he could into the woods;
Molly took off like a bullet.

Sims propped the door open and went back to
work, "Check out the toys on the couch and see

what else you can think of." John picked up and set down three different night scopes and two night glasses used to mark targets in pitch dark.

Sims came out on the north side this time with a .223 rifle with a night scope on it, "We can use this to check for lemonade." John gave a look, "Really?" "Well you been dragging your ass and it is getting dark, so yes." John looked at the scope on the .223, "Where is the one with all the lighting modes." "Well, that is on my kit and we don't move it on and off; years now right where it belongs." John said, "Can we check for lemonade with that?"

Sims gave John a serious look, "Are you serious?" "Look we may have trouble making these things out. So, anything we have to zero in on them is what we need."

Sims got closer; really serious now, "Wait a minute; you really don't think these things are animals do you?" John looked Sims in the eyes, "Never seen anything move like these things do, so I have my doubts." Molly came back in and broke the moment. She dropped the ball at Sims feet and sat there waiting. She was covered in leaves and dirt. John looked at Sims, "Where the hell did you throw that?"

John cleaned up Molly as fast as he could and got to the suite; it was well into dusk. He laid out all the toys on the couch against the south wall. The fridge was on the same wall near the back door. There were comfortable smaller upholstered chairs across from the couch, as was the other door leading out onto the walk. To the right of the door, on the lower wall, was the security panel; the alarm indicator was green.

Sims had gone back to his house to retrieve his most precious item. John walked out the door, went to the middle of walk way and looked down on the open grass field leading down the hill to Sims' house.

John heard Sims coming up the steps and opened the back door for him. He came in sideways with his desert camouflaged, highly customized, sniper kit against his right side. He and John got a beer and went front and center on the walk. Sims took a long thirsty pull on his beer, burped, and said, "How do we start?" "Well, just like recon Sims, we look for movement."

There was nothing going on; it was full dark. John was wondering if these things were playing games; trying to make him sound insane. At 8:30pm John went to pee off the northwest corner of the walk; there was a large funnel there that fed down to the flower beds. He had just reached full stream when he turned his head to look at the shooting range.

From up there he could see the last two stations, the woods, and lots of lemonade, "Sims! Get over here."

John had holstered his weapon without peeing all over himself just as Sims got there, "What?" John pointed, "Look on the north side of the last two stations; you see all that?" Sims moved passed him to the middle of the west side walk, "Ok, see what?" "All the movement, the light moving between the trees" Sims gave John a sad look. John exploded, "Bullshit don't you look at me like that. There has to be a reason you can't see them? The doctors told me the color registration in my eyes would be jacked for years. That is why I had you bring your scope."

Sims was about to say something, but John had walked back to the door. He reached inside and grabbed Sims' rifle and returned to Sims' "Look through this and flip through the modes." Sims slowly took the rifle, "There is no reason looking through this will allow me to see anything different."

Sims shouldered the weapon sited the area in question and saw nothing, "John I am telling you this ain't gonna make any difference." He moved his head to find the mode switch and pushed it, "This is the second mode called starrrrr...shit what the hell is that."

John put his elbows on the railing looking west, "Now Master Sergeant Sims answer your own question; I am dying to hear what you come up with; would you like to start with the color; how about lemonade?" Sims looked up from the scope, "I need another beer." John said, "I'll get it for you; continue through the modes we need to note each one. We will need Glenn to sort this out."

They spent the next couple of hours using all the night vision gear to see how they reacted to the "peculiarities" they were seeing. On the low light and pitch dark setting Sims saw nothing. On the starlight and enhanced modes he saw them. On the enhanced setting he felt the extra contrast led him to feel there was something else out there with them.

John was cataloguing all the results and they were talking about what they could be. Sims took his rifle out the back once more to verify something and they were gone. He came back in and John was gone. He went out on the east side walk and found John; all of them had migrated to the east field. They were really moving fast and Sims got to see them dive into the ground.

John turned to go, "You cover me I am going down there." Sims looked at him, "You sure? Lemonade can sting your eyes." "I got to make sure someone is not projecting this shit into the compound for some reason." "You mean like holograms?" "Yup; or drive in movies." "Not this again, did you eat Beer Nuts at the drive in movies?" John went down the stairs.

Molly met him at the kitchen doors; she had to go, but was afraid. John walked with her to the cement deck and she quickly did her thing; she wasn't going to chance the lawn area. John understood her now; he would hose it off later.

He put her back to bed in the kitchen and grabbed his big mag-lite and headed out the front doors. He went across the wood deck, down the stairs and out on to the lawn. He flashed the light so Sims could pick him up.

When John got close to where he thought they had seen them he called Sims on his cell, "Where do I go?" "You got lemonade ahead ten yards, four degrees northeast." John started moving in that direction; he took three steps and suddenly found himself in a pocket of cold air; it really creeped him out. He walked faster and it was gone. He expected to be seeing the things by now. Sims whispering for some reason, "You are starting to draw attention." John walked even faster for about twenty feet more. He felt a warming sensation as he went; he thought he was sweating from the situation. "You walked right through three of them; they didn't react at all.

You might be right, they may be fakes. There was no indication of shadow or an external light source; or any reflection …nothing."

John switched on his mag-lite and pointed it back where he had been, "Anything different." Yup I can't see shit; turn it off." John waved him off, "Look around the edges of the glare to see if something shows." "On it." John swept his light around in a slow left to right manner. He saw something strange and was going to take another pass when he jumped out of his skin; Sims had fired a round from his rifle. John spun around, "What the hell; how about some warning!"

Sims was still staring at the spot he where he had fired; no movement; no nothing; absolutely nothing; and that was the problem. He scanned the area he saw the yellow guys moving and the ground around them, John, his light and its glare on the ground. He scanned back to the spot where he fired, and nothing, like a black out, "I thought I saw something, but it turned out to be nothing; absolutely nothing at all, just a hole in the air." John looked up at Sims then at his phone, "What?" Sims returning the scope to the spot saw something he didn't understand. The hole in the air diffused like smoke, and he could see everything he couldn't see around it to begin with; for a split second he thought he saw it move away.

"I don't know what I am seeing anymore; we've been at this for five hours and seven beers. It's almost midnight and you got me going to Knoxville in the morning; we still need to discuss that."

John made it back up to the widow's suite where Sims was sitting on the couch with a beer in his hand, staring at the floor. His rifle was standing near the door. They looked at each other with equally baffled looks.

Sims took a drink of his beer and looked at John, "What was going on out there?" John shrugged and sat in one of the chairs, "Now they are moving south. The alarm always trips from the kitchen service door on the south side." "Well, I could go around and shoot their asses; oh, no I can't cuz they're not made of anything; but we can see them, and they move, and sheeeeeit! What are they?"

John tried to stay in control to calm Sims down, "Look I will get on the phone with Glenn and see if he has some ideas that don't include having us committed. I would like to see if we can record them somehow."

Sims stood up, finished his beer, and threw it in the trash, "John you really got to focus on something. If these things are setting off the alarm, then they want in; Molly's got this figured out." John spun around, "What, she is scared shitless." "Exactly, she knows there ain't nothing she can do about it. I am going to bed. I's a two hour drive to Knoxville; call me on the road. Good night."

Chapter Thirteen:

Day Two

1:00am

Dream Room

Hart Compound

At 1:00am John was still awake. Molly was out like a light on her side of the dream room. John kept running the night back in his mind; he felt there was something they missed.

He had learned a technique in therapy to help him understand his dreams; the technique followed the senses. First, what had you seen? He went through each of the events, but focused on the part when he and Sims were separated. He walked a hundred and fifty yards to get to where they were seeing the yellow things, as he approached he saw nothing strange, ground, grass, low light from the widow's suite, nothing moving. He turned on his mag-light and saw what?

He had just started to sweep when he was startled by the shot. What did he see on the sweep? John was staring at the doors on the east wall. He went over and looked out to where he had been.

He unconsciously moved his hand like he had the mag-lite. He turned his body following the beam of light in his mind. John was scanning when he saw a black spot. In this case he was focused on Molly's back; he realized he lost the beam in the black and it resumed after several feet on the right. *What was that? The same kind of thing Sims shot at?*

He played back the sounds. There was the shot; what did Sims say he was shooting at, "I thought I saw something, but it turned out to be nothing; nothing at all, a hole in the air."

What did he feel? Scary movie scared, like something was going to pop up out of nowhere. He felt better when he could talk to Sims on his cell. He got his bearings from Sims; but didn't want to go. He started to walk and it was suddenly cold; really cold; it scared him and he walked fast to move away. Warm? He felt warmth about half way through his retreat from the cold. Sims said, "You walked right through three of them."

Smells were last; fresh air, grass, light oil from the weapons and scopes on his hand, and on the mag-lite. John leaned his head back as if looking at the ceiling, eyes shut, but still in line with Molly. He let his head lean back to the doors; *cold should smell fresh, crisp…not like a dead body. There was nothing out there before dark, Molly and I looked…frozen dead things don't smell at all.*

John went to his bed, it was 1:20am now, and he adjusted his pillows and sat up against the head board. He did not want to believe the evidence, *there are yellow ones and black ones; the black ones were nasty.*

At 3:10am John was launched from his bed grabbing at his chest screaming. He landed in the middle of the bed on his hands and knees; breathing like he had sprinted an entire marathon. John had to get his breathing down. Molly did as she had been trained; she climbed into his lap and pressed her body into his chest. John acknowledged her with a strong and long hug his face on her back right at the base of her neck; his breathing started to even out.

John had to clean himself up. He had emptied his bowels at the end of the dream. He got in the shower and fought back his anguish.

John had just been impaled by the tail of a demonic being; gross smelling things that hunted him each month. They surround him, gnashing their teeth; mouths like lions with the teeth to match, their faces looked like hideous men covered in earth with long mangy hair.

The craziest part was John could not out run them; every time he was about to escape, wings would rip out of their backs. They would swoop down, catch him, and throw him down hundreds of feet to the ground. Finally, they would huddle around him, and the same one would slam his stinger right through his chest; John could see the delight on their faces. He wondered if it was because he was dead, or that they got to kill him again in a few days.

John got dry, took his bedding and threw it down the chute. The bed was now covered with nothing but plastic. He put on his robe and went and sat in the middle of Molly's bed. He sat facing his bed with his eyes looking out the glass doors.

John and Molly had one last thing to do. He scooted back so his back was against the wall. Molly came and sat on his lap facing west, and then she leaned into John so her head was on his right shoulder and her breath would be on his neck below his ear. John put his right arm around her and put his left hand on her heart.

John could feel her steady breathing on his neck; her heartbeat with his left hand. She brought him all the way back to normal in about five minutes.

She got down, faced him, and sat down as if saying, *Ok, you're good, so what's next.* John hadn't thought of that; he smiled, *The Coffee hole?* John stood up,

"Molly, let's get some coffee!" Molly barked, *damn straight, goin' for a ride*

Chapter Fourteen

.

4:20am

Coffee Hole

West of Jonesborough, TN

John turned left as the gate closed behind him. He drove on for a couple hundred yards, "Lights on. NAV, Coffee west of Jonesborough." Smiling He turned and looked at Molly, "Thank you little girl, you saved me again." Molly put her head in his lap and he scratched her ears all the way there.

As they were pulling up John slowed way down; Adam and Lil' Joe were standing outside of the Coffee Hole on the right side of the door. He wondered if something was wrong. It looked like a pretty intense conversation. John decided that his need for coffee outweighed their need for privacy. He pulled in.

John and Molly got out; John led the way, and Molly fell in behind him. They approached the guys, "Hey what's goin' on?" Adam held both arms in front of him; a stop gesture, "You don't want to go in there." "Why not?" Lil Joe pinched his nose, "Gas leak." He looked inside and looked back at Joe, "Hoss is in there how bad could it be; where is Phu?" Adam put his right hand on John's shoulder, "Real bad; Hoss is the gas leak. Phu is in there trying to save his dough."

"John had had enough non-sense. He figured they were still messing with him. He had already died tonight; a fart wasn't going kill him. He opened the door and went in; Molly moved behind Adam and Joe. The door hadn't even begun to close before John came blasting out, "Geez, what the fuck is that? Are you telling me that is just one of his farts? Jesus help us if he shits his pants! Phu is gonna have to bury that dough."

John looked over at Molly, "You! You could have blocked the door." He knew when she was grinning and she was grinning now."

John went back to the Polaris and grabbed his breath mints, stuffed one up each nostril, gave a mock smile to Molly and headed back in.

Hoss waved; he was smiling like a hen that had just laid a double yoker. Phu stuck his head out from around the back as John grabbed the whole pot of coffee and three cups. Phu nodded his approval; John noticed he had smeared raspberry filling under his nose.

John came out, "I will probably have to burn this jacket. At least I won't have to de-skunk the dog." He could swear Molly giggled.

They all got into his Polaris. Molly would not yield shotgun so the guys climbed in the back. John handed the coffee to Adam and cups to Lil' Joe. He reached to the dash, turned a knob; he and Molly's seats turned towards each other until they were facing the boys in the back; Adam poured the coffee.

Lil' Joe started the obvious conversation, "You know I never thought about this 'til now; I think there is great potential in weaponizing his ass. We could hang his ass out of a chopper and let him drop one on Isis; he could take out entire villages in one pass."

John was more contemplative, "Does he have neighbors? Oh my God, a cesspool; he could take out the entire waters supply. His fart fan must take up the whole ceiling. He must have to re-paint his bathroom every week.

"Is he married? Who could live like that?" Joe leaned over and whispered, "Thank God she don't come down here with him." John almost hit his head on the roof, "No! You gotta be kidding!" John was laughing his ass off now.

Adam was shaking his head with a sad look on his face. John just catching his breath, "Since high school? No wonder you guys are brain damaged." They all laughed and Molly barked. Adam pointed toward the shop; Phu was giving the all clear sign. They went in started on Hoss.

John and Molly made it home and had some breakfast. John made oatmeal; he added some of the granola from yesterday with cut up apple. Molly inspected what was going on and decided on a grass fed burger patty on her kibble; *oatmeal was for puppies.*

Molly had the right idea; she got in her bed and was gone. John hadn't slept more than four hours the last two days, but he had calls to make.

He called Sims first. Sims answered with, "How was your night?" John let out a long sigh, "I died, then woke up went had some coffee; you?" "Pretty much the same thing except I didn't sleep well. Now I have to drive two hours before I can wake up."

Sims, ever sarcastic, sounded almost sad. John had been concerned about Sims, "You think of anything last night to explain our evening?" "Yup, I didn't tell you last night, but I think there is another something hanging with the lemonade boys." John half smiled, "I think you're right. I figure there are black ones as well; is that what you felt?" Sims was quiet for a few seconds, "That's what I was shooting at; a hole in the air. I saw it diffuse into nothing like it was smoke blowing away." John was quiet now, "I think I walked right through one of them; it was cold as hell and smelled like road kill."

Sims changed the subject; he seemed even more subdued, "I know I am going to talk with Gavin and his security guys about prepping for Zhang whoever. I know Confidante like the back of my hand. I worked with Gavin and Jess at the start, but I still don't know where all this technology came from. Looking at you guys I didn't figure you invented it, so how? I asked Gavin and Jess at different times, and they said I had to hear it from you. Do you guys still feel I am an outsider, or a risk?

There it was; the thing John could never figure out. He couldn't explain why Sims acted like he wasn't part of the group; like a hired hand. John had blown it and had hurt Sims by his own stupidity.

"Sims I am so sorry. I thought Glenn had filled you in on everything, I thought from day one you were a trusted member of the group. You would not be anywhere near here if you were not one of us.

"I feel so shitty that I didn't sit down and talk with you personally. Now it is so obvious, I should have known better. Nick and I are brothers and we grew up with Glenn, our approval was built in. I will call ahead and talk to Jess; she should be the one to tell you all about it. I will tell you this, this whole group started from a bar fight and a junkie. I am really sorry I have been such an ass this whole time."

Sims was quiet, "Well it takes a big man to admit I've been right all along; I been calling you an ass for a long time and now you finally see it. Thanks John, I can't wait to hear who kicked your ass way back when. Obviously Nick was the junkie?" They both laughed and they were back just as before...it was a man thing. John joined Molly for a nap.

Chapter Fifteen:

10:10am

Confidante

Knoxville, TN

Two hours later Sims was in a conference room with Gavin and Jess. They discussed how they would work for the next two days, and then told Sims they reserved a very nice room where he could rest.

Sims looked at each one of them, "What's going on?" Jess stood up, "John said that you guys worked late fixing some problems with the front yard lighting, and you were up very late. He said you worked five hours and seven beers too long. So he suggested you get a couple of hours sleep.

I am to take you somewhere relaxing so I could fill you in on the military side of the business." Sims, a little embarrassed, "That sounds perfect so now what?" "Leave your SUV here and I will have someone check you in. We will come for you at

4:30pm for drinks and slanderous gossip." Sims nodded, "Can't wait."

Sims was ready and waiting when the car came for him. He was surprised when it dropped him off at a Cracker Barrel restaurant.

He loved the biscuits and the Maker's Mark was good as well. Jess was at a table along a wall decorated with all kinds of farming tools. She waved him over and they ordered drinks.

Sims looked around, the place was almost full; waitresses running all over everywhere, "Sure is loud in here." Jess leaned in, "Exactly, impossible to eves drop on our gossip." Sims sat back and nodded; his bourbon arrived along with Jess's Seagram's; he started to relax.

Jess Williams was a tall brunette, with brown eyes that were bright with intelligence. Her legs were a little long for her, but they were balanced out by her torso and long hair. She was attractive in a plain Jane kind of way. She wore custom tailored men's business suits with expensive shoes. For tonight she had lost the jacket and tie.

She may have had some Italian in her; she was quite animated when she talked. What Sims liked the day he met her was that she was real; and really funny.

While they enjoyed their meal they had done some catching up and some trash talking about the early days at Confidante. They ordered coffee and desert so they could stay for a while without anyone rushing them from their table. Sims took a sip of his coffee, "Now what is this about a bar fight and a junkie?"

Jess said, "I am going to tell you this as I heard from Nick one time when he and John came to see me in Boston to discuss my junkie friend.

"So, back in 2006, John, Nick and Glenn decided to celebrate before they left San Dimas, California behind. They all hated the place. They had no fond memories of living in California. It was also John's twenty-first birthday, and the money from his settlement had finally been deposited in his account.

"John kept four million in the states, and put the remaining forty-five million off shore. The lawyers and litigation finance company got the rest of the sixty-three million." Sims choked on his coffee, "Shit! That is a lot of money for a kid to have?" Jess smiled, "His legal team kicked California's ass. They could have appealed for more, but John just wanted his life back; but he made sure his mother was put away.

"They had decided to party at Glenn's place. They had done a great job of killing brain cells, and they were hungry. They needed to call ahead for pizza and grab some beers. Right around the corner from them was Clete's Liquor Store who shared their east wall with The Pizza Place; one stop shopping.

"They decided to get the pizza first. When they arrived the pizza was almost done so they just stood at the bar and waited. They waved at John and brought the pizza to the register. As John walked over he heard someone yell out, "Look it's that fucking retard Hart!" Sims chimed in, "Oh it's on now!" Jess was nodding.

"Nick explained that most of the time John would have skulked away smiling, embarrassed, but not anymore. He realized he was not guilty. Not a retard, he had shown the entire state that it was the child abuse. Today would be different. He located his heckler and said, "Fuck you asshole, and watch your mouth there are kids in here." John turned back to pay the check.

"Nick told me the story using an assholes verses the good guys theme. So it went like this; asshole number one, the heckler, was stunned for a second; then lost his mind. Stomping across the restaurant he was about to grab John by the shoulder when John spun and hit him right between the eyes with a quick left and down he went.

"Glenn laughed and yelled, "Clean-up on aisle five!" Sims fell back in his chair, "Go Johnny boy." "Just as Glenn patted John on the back for a job well done, he was grabbed from behind by asshole number two.

"Now you guys call Glenn Sasquatch right?" Sims nodded yes. "Well maybe this is why. Glenn turned into the guy, broke his grip, and took him by the throat with one hand and the belt buckle with the other. He picked the guy up and carried him out to the parking lot and dumped him." At this point Sims was giggling. Jess smiled a wicked smile, "We're just getting started. While John watched Glenn drop the guy on his back, he was tackled by asshole number three.

"This guy hits John square in the chest; down he went. On the way down John turns so he can land on the guy. But this guy was fast. He got on top of John before he could do anything. He was just about to pop John when the guy disappears. Nick said he horse collared the guy, put him in choke hold and dragged him to Glenn who was just coming back in.

"Sasquatch takes him from Nick; he grabs him by the shirt collar and a back pocket of his jeans and walked him out like a dog; then kicked him right in the ass, landing him in the parking lot." Sims was clapping now; people were looking at them; they didn't care. They refreshed their coffee.

"Nick said John didn't say much about it. Glenn told Nick later that he put his arm around John and said, "Don't tell me that didn't feel good." John looked down at asshole number one sitting on the floor; his face covered with bloody napkins and told him, "Shoulda done that years ago.""

Chapter Sixteen:

6:00pm

Cracker Barrel

Knoxville, TN

Jess took a sip of her coffee, "Well, now we move on to the Junkie part of the story. The owner gave them their pizza for free, and the people cheered as they left. As they stepped outside the sheriffs were cuffing the three assholes. When they were done, they came over and cuffed them." Sims mouth fell open, "What! Why did they do that?" Jess grinned at him, "Good thing they did.

"While they were waiting for the reports from witnesses at the scene, our boys had to give their statements of what went down; while they watched the officers eat their pizza. As they progressed the main topic of conversation became John's overwhelming defeat of the State of California. Two of the officers on duty had run-ins with John at the various schools he attended. They noted how different he was. John explained being off the medications allowed him to act normal.

"They placed them in a two cell lock up. John hadn't noticed anybody in the other cell until he heard mumbling. There was a guy lying on his left side facing the cell doors. He looked like he was a sleep; his grey hoodie was pulled over his head. That was my friend Craig Battle.

"I met him in Boston, we were put together at M.I.T. by a group of companies that were looking to develop products. Their plan was to allow the top minds in the country to run wild with their money.

"They would give grants based on merit. I came over from Michigan and Craig from Stanford. We created a variety of gadgets for auto industry and made some money.

"We decided to really work together rather than the support mode we were in. Our first major project was a sensor array, and software that really improved the diagnostic abilities of the CPUs of automobiles. We scored big time on that one. That led to a few other smaller enhancements that paid very well.

"Later we met with an investment group. We were interviewed individually and together. They asked what we would create if we had all the money in the world. I guess our answers were close enough that they wanted to sign us as a team to work on Craig's dream."

"They felt he could not bring about the realization of his dream without the ideas I had presented. It was a team or nothing. We took it.

We got personal bonuses and a sizable grant; so we went to work. Craig's ideas were beyond my expertise in physics, but I could restate his thoughts in a way that he found clarifying. I could see a huge challenge in the software end; I would have to create completely new and complex code to pull it off.

Sims noticed that Jess was becoming more serious; emotional now, "We were into it quite a ways when Craig began to show up late looking all messed up. He seemed obsessed with tiny little details. He knew a way of making it work. I would ask him, "What is it? How is it going to work?" He would say, "It is like recycling lightning. It's like a Nano-collider on a chip; it will just keep pumping out the power. It is so fast; my brain has to keep up."

Jess paused looking in her empty cup, "I figured out he was using meth. I tried to talk to him, but he continued to get worse; it was eating his brain.

"I know he got really close to finalizing his ideas, but he couldn't get that one thing; his mind was leaving him. Finally, I packed him up and sent him home.

"I tried to salvage the grant with an idea I had, but it didn't work out. I worked with other R&D firms made a lot of money; but I never stopped thinking about what he said at the airport, "It is Cern in a cell phone." Sims looked puzzled, "Cern?" Yes, it's a place in Switzerland where the world's most prominent Super Collider is."

She stopped and kind of shook it off, "I need a drink." They moved to another part of the restaurant and sat by the bar. Sims got a beer and Jess had some white wine. She was quiet while she sipped. Sims asked, "Did you fall for this guy?" "No, I just miss the absolute genius he was; it's such a waste!" Sims nodded, "But you saved his dream; yes?" She brightened up. "Yes."

She let out a long sigh, "When John found him he was mumbling the same things. He was a mess. He was picked up wondering around in the hills near his house in La Verne, California. He told the police he lived in San Dimas and they dropped him on the Sheriffs. He had only been in his cell three hours when our boys were jailed for fist-a-cuffs.

"John had moved to where he could see Craig better; he was trying to hear what he was saying. Craig sat up real fast and freaked John. Craig just kept staring at him until John said, "What's up?" John said Craig's eyes were darting all over the place when Craig said, "I am pretty messed up but I gotta keep workin.'" John asked him what he was working on and he started in with the collider deal.

"John asked another way. He told Craig he was going to make millions in the burner phone industry; Craig sat up straight and asked him, "Why make burners when you could leap frog the entire technology by ten years? That got John's attention.

"Glenn tried asking more questions but Craig passed out." Sims looked Jess in the eye, "That is what goes on underground at Confidante?" She grinned, "Yes, but we are even better now that we fully understand. John formed a plan and it worked. The first thing they had to do was get Craig's brain back and get all his thoughts in order; second was finding me.

"First thing they got Craig on a good diet, exercise, lots of sleep and almost zero drugs. He would slip now and then; that was also when there were a couple hours on clarity.

"Craig audio recorded all our work and brainstorming sessions. At home he would talk to the recorder for hours. John went through all the recordings they could find with Craig while taking notes. He would note where Craig engaged and where he lost it. They put together everything they could then they came looking for me in Boston.

"While John and Glenn came to see me Nick was working with the lawyers setting up contingency plans for helping Craig realize what he had started.

"They brought me paper work that in essence gave me technology power of attorney. I was impressed how they worked for me and Craig; John was acting as an advocate not a venture capitalist.

"We came to terms after I had talked to Craig and learned of his trust in John. The first contract was about finding out if there was an idea that could work; after that we would re-assess.

"John arranged for me to work in the same lab Craig and I had worked in. He got me a couple of researchers and assistants. After a year I felt we were close to finding exactly what Craig had pictured in his mind, but I was stuck.

"John pulled some strings and the next thing I know I am observing the operations of the super collider at Cern; which is near Geneva, Switzerland. I was there four months before the light came on. I was struck by how much momentum there was left after they finished a test. They would get the particles up to speed to verify they could reach the required speed without destroying whatever particles they were working on. The particles would continue at high velocity for a long time. I realize we weren't going to smash atoms we just needed to generate power.

"In theory a small boost of power could keep the particle moving forever; if movement can convert to power a collider in a cell phone would be just what the doctor ordered. Let the battery charge itself using a little to gain a lot."

"Sims was gawking at her, "Shit the kid is a genius." "Was; when I was at Cern Craig overdosed and died.

"John had his lawyers execute the terms of Craig's agreement; his family will be receiving a percentage of sales checks for as long as there are sales. The initial payment to his mother came when we signed with General Rouse and the boys; she got eleven million to get things started." Sims was smiling, "Anybody else would have kept the money; the mother would have never known what went on with a top secrete project."

Jess nodded, "He did right by me as well; way beyond expectations." Sims smiled, "Yes, I hear that you are the proud owner of a ground breaking new company at the fore front of battery technology. Soon the electric car will be a true value. Never charge; never replace, wow what a sales slogan. John knows how to build an empire." Jess did a mock bow, "I have a project of my own that will need an owner soon." Sims was nodding, "Pay it forward sister."

Jess sat up and re-engaged, "The second part was the icing on the cake; it was my deal. Instead of putting the collider on a chip we made a mesh from a super conductive material that absorbs all the energy around it. In actuality it would retrieve all the energy lost in using the phone.

"We put the collider in a mesh that surrounds the entire inside of the works. The phone feeds the mesh. So the Nano-collider became like a freeway with a million on ramps. When we need a ton of power, we do what Cern does, we accelerate the particles; thus our boost mode.

"The boost mode basically allows our phones the power and signal gain to become a highly powered satellite phone. Our devices never run out of power." Sims smiled, "So every G.I. can now have a satellite phone to call for air strikes or help." Jess nodded, "Or to call home."

Sims let his mind wander, "Troops with mini drones on line all the time; never ambushed." Jess held up her hands, "We have sixty projects in the pipeline and we have enhanced our existing equipment in several technology areas. Mister Sims, we are bad ass, no bullshit people; and that's the story of the bar fight and the junkie."

Chapter Seventeen

10:30am

Master Suite

Hart Compound

John was awakened by Molly; he rolled over looked at the clock, he had gotten about five hours sleep. Molly was really pressing the issue. He went to the back of the walk in closet, slid back the mirrored section and keyed in his code. The wall slid back, revealed an elevator and he and Molly were going down. He came out the closet in the entry way in front, killed the security, opened the front doors, and out they went.

Molly went in at least five different places; she sniffed all over where he had been last night. He figured Sims was at Confidante meeting with Jess and Gavin by now. He called Molly they headed for the kitchen.

He was starving and made a full breakfast. John and Molly ate the first half pound of bacon standing up, then the other half with their meal.

John made really good coffee, but he wished he was with The Coffee Hole Gang; *that would be a bad ass t-shirt*. He cleaned up, got dressed for an active day.

He went down to the kitchen and grabbed his phone. He needed to let Nick know what he and Sims discovered. He would call Glenn once he and Nick had talked; Nick was in charge of weird shit. Nick sounded tired; he had been flying around a lot lately.

John and Nick went over Nick's meeting with General Rouse; Rouse was concerned but the NSA was not; they felt Zhang was nothing to worry about. Rouse presented the info that Glenn had put together; they wanted to know the source before they would even look into it.

Rouse made it clear to the leadership there, if he had to come back to the NSA after something had gone south, he was bringing a hatchet; heads were going to roll.

Nick said Sims had called about Confidante from his meeting with Jess and Gavin; Nick told Sims Rouse is going to help on the government employee thing he just needs to fund it.

John and Nick decided in the long run it would be cheaper to give them company cars and write off the leases. Uncle Sam would pay anyway, no need to request funds. Nick would follow up with Sims.

Finally John asked, "Where are you; doesn't sound like you're at home?" Nick sat back in his booth at a diner in Rockland, Maine, "I am in Rockland for the second annual celebration of the Norlander Park Project. I am having some lunch."

John was quiet for a moment then said, "What? The what?" "Remember when Glenn wanted the Iron Wood for the beams to ground the compound? We won the bid because we built the city a park." John searching his brain, "You mean the big, heavy ass wood that framed the main house and widow's suite?" "That's the stuff."

John sat forward, put his head in his hands, elbows on the table, "That shit required special cranes and teams to make it work; that was one of the most time consuming and costly parts of the whole project. I didn't know about the park." Well there was another buyer that really wanted that stuff and we thought park instead of cash; we wrote the park off to charity."

John sat up shaking his head, "Well, I hope you're not in a hurry to get to the park cuz I got some weird stuff to tell you." Nick sat quietly listening sipping his coffee until John mentioned the yellow and black phantoms hanging around the compound.

Nick suddenly was very interested, "Wait a minute, you felt them; one was ice cold; they smelled like a dead animal, and then Sims shot one?" "Yup, we both saw them, and Sims saw me walk through them."

Nick stood up, threw some money on the table, and walked out to his rental car. He sat with a concerned look on his face while he listened to the Molly portion of the story, "Son of a bitch John, I think I need to look into a couple of things; give me two days; I'll call you back." Nick hung up.

John was actually looking at his phone wondering what the hell Nick was gonna do. John didn't know Nick negotiated the final transactions and shipping of the wood. Nick had heard some strange tales throughout the process.

Chapter Eighteen

12:10pm

Jonesborough, TN

John called Molly and they went out the south kitchen door where the Polaris was parked. John checked the door for damage, and found nothing was amiss; Molly was sitting by the car door. He looked at her and she looked away, "Molly, come sniff" he pointed to the door; she looked away.

He took out his handkerchief and wiped the inside edges of the jams and pressed it to his nose; not a good smell. He opened the car doors and they got in. John took the handkerchief and started to move it towards Molly's nose; she showed her teeth and gave John a look, *get that damn thing away from me!*

He rolled down his window and threw it on the ground and showed her his empty hands. He then extended the back of the right hand to her muzzle and she licked it; he started the Polaris.

As they drove toward Jonesborough, John had two reactions to ponder. Molly's reactions were pretty clear, *Bad things at the kitchen door stupid; the alarms have been going off for weeks; fix this shit.* Nick's reaction on the other hand was very cryptic and unsettling.

He was going into town to see Sheriff Jeffery Barlow at the courthouse on Main Street. John wanted to know if there had been reports of vandals recently. He also wanted to check if there were any problems reported with his night shooting. It was 12:30, just past lunch time maybe Jeff would still like to join him.

Jeff had been Sheriff long before John and his minions had ransacked the land west of town. Jeff was forty years old, with sandy brown hair. He was five foot ten inches, medium build, with brown eyes; his hair style was 1950's lawman.

Jeff had a good sense of humor and could shoot pretty well. He had to safety check the shooting range and noise specifications. The high foliage and the woods dampened much of the noise and the nearest anything was town.

John stuck his head in the door, "Mind if I bust in here without an appointment?" Jeff smiled, "Hey stranger, coming down from the mountains for supplies?" "No just have some business to discuss with you and thought you might be hungry." Jeff hesitated looking at his desk, "Hell why not, this stuff isn't going anywhere; No one asks the sheriff out to lunch anymore. They just want to know when you gonna fix this, or stop that."

They went round the back of the station; Molly and John got in the police cruiser. "Where to sheriff? You pick it I'll pay it." "Well the best lunch is at the sports bar over a ways." "That sounds good." They talked about shooting and Molly until they got seated and their food arrived. John had brought along a chew stick to keep Molly busy in the car while they ate.

Jeff took a sip of his coke, "So business?" "I've been wondering if anyone has said anything about noise from the range" Jeff looked confused for a second, "The range?" John was almost sorry he had asked; seemed like he forgot, "My gun range; you signed off on the safety and noise?" Jeff turned red, "Oh, sorry I forgot all about that. Nobody has said a word. Why?" John smiled, "No worries, I have had some weird activity at the compound and wondered if there had been reports of vandalism anywhere a bouts?" Jeff thought a minute, "So you think maybe someone getting back at you for some noise?" "Really, I am reaching; trying to eliminate all the possibilities."

"Quite frankly John I don't think anybody ever thinks about your place. No one ever talks about it that I know of. So, no I don't think you have a town problem. Shit, I forgot I did your inspection."

They drove back to the courthouse and as they were getting out of the cruiser John asked, "You know Phu, Hoss, Joe and Adam; they said they been friends around here since high school?" Jeff smiled, "Now those are some funny boys. They love to play tricks on everyone; but they're good people."

John thought he had them now, "So do they play the Bonanza trick on everyone?" "I don't know what you mean." John frowning, "You know Hoss, Lil Joe and Adam; the Ponderosa, Virginia City?" "John you've been acting weird all day; you OK out there on your own?" John's head fell, "I am fine, thanks for coming to lunch. We'll get you back out to the range and see if you can beat your score." Jeff looked at him again like he was crazy. John and Molly left; Molly was excited and John was mumbling.

Chapter Nineteen

2:10pm

Rockland, Maine

Nick had found his way to City Hall and the Rockland Historical Department. He had been waiting to see the historian on duty, Dorothy Wickem. Ms. Wickem seemed to be a chatty one; simple yes and no questions answered with everything but yes or no.

Dorothy was just what Nick wanted, someone who knew everything and was dying to tell it. Nick thought if he doubted her info she would tell every detail; making sure no one would question her integrity. He only hoped she knew what he needed to know.

It was finally his turn. He was about to state his business when Dorothy said, "Mr. Hart how good to see you. I am so glad you made it to the park again this year. You and your associates have made such a big difference in this town." Nick nodded, "I need your help. Do you remember the events that led to our building Norlander Park?" Dorothy looked around, "Well, Mr. Hart you should know better than anyone." "Yes, but do you know; because if you do then I can save a ton of time explaining what I need." Dorothy still thinking it was a test, "Well I am game fire away."

Nick was thinking, *I could die here just trying to ask a question,* "Ok, I need to know the story of how the wood came to be for sale, who the other bidders were, and the providence of the wood." Dorothy was now looking somewhat baffled, "You mean the providence of the Norlander house, Mr. Hart; you purchased the Norlander's house." Nick was about to lose it when it made sense. The pile of wood was again a house in Jonesborough; Nick didn't like how that made him feel.

Nick asked if she knew the story of the house. Once again she was a bit confused or playing confused so she could correct him again. Dorothy said, "There is the history of the house and there is the story of the house and all that was Norlander."

Nick felt he had lost control of this inquiry, "I want to know both the history and the lore." He felt that would give her license to gossip. She cocked her head and said, "Why now; after you have purchased the house, are you dissatisfied with the house?" Nick looked left then right and lowered his voice, "The house is now part of a large military research and development laboratory. The government must know where every piece of the facility came from and how it was made; also, any previous use with which it was tasked." She left him abruptly and was gone for some time.

Dorothy returned with a heavy nine by twelve envelope and a folded piece of paper. She handed him the envelope, "History." She handed him the paper, "Lore." Nick nodded and left. He called the bed and breakfast he stayed in last night and booked a room.

Nick called Glenn so he could pull his building notes and give him what info he had. He hoped he could do it without getting Glenn involved. Glenn's notes were in his computer; he brought them up, "What are you looking for." "I am in Rockland for the second annual celebration of Norlander Park; I need info to help fill out this history brochure being made by the history lady. I need what pictures you have and if you know who we out bid for the wood; down here we bought a house not wood." Glenn was looking, "It is a house once again Master Nick."

"I got pictures of the old house intact and close ups of all the wood pieces; the broker was told not to reveal the bidders, and I quote, "ever." "Can you put that together and get it to my laptop; I am on a tight schedule, thanks."

Nick wanted to find a particular diner he ate in three years ago; the crazy old man he had talked to back then didn't sound so crazy now.

After forty-five minutes of driving around, Nick found the diner near Jameson Point. He sat down; while he waited he opened the folded paper, "Annabel Gibson" aka "Gibby" and a local phone number.

Nick started to open the envelope when the waitress came for his order. He asked her about the old man. Nick described him and pointed to where he had talked with him, and told her what he was going on about. Without taking his order she left; after five minutes she came back with the old man; he was the owner of the diner.

Chapter Twenty

John was looking at photos of the construction. He showed a presentation chronicling the compound build at the group's completion party. It was a BBQ for all the workers and staff; a shooting tournament, with live bands and lots of security.

He found the ground breaking photos and sorted the file to start there. He clicked through until he came to the raising of the timber framed walls.

He went back and found several photos of the wood laid out on the ground as they would appear when assembled. There were markings on each piece where they would connect; match the markings build the wall and so on. There was a close up of one series of markings in the middle of a long beam; white chalk was rubbed into the markings to make them readable. The markings seemed to form a phrase; but not in English but looked almost Arabic. There were markings on each end as well; *Maybe a door mantel?*

He called Glenn, "Hey, you hunt down our boy Zhang Jie?" Glenn sounded like he was working while he was talking, "Almost, working on it right now.

"Did Nick tell you about the NSA?" John grinned, "I heard he almost gave you up for one of those cool phones they have." "Never happen; Nick would never do that; those phones would have to be a lot better than the shit they use." John laughed out loud, "But he would give you up if the price was right?" "For the right woman? In a heartbeat."

Glenn didn't care for the NSA and their arrogance, "I think the NSA fails to do their homework. Right now Zhang and several of his friends are leading them down the path; the NSA thinks all their deeds are done by someone Zhang and the boys created; a Russian named Matvey. John almost yawned, "So what's the plan now God of all cyber?"

"Well, being the nice guy that I am, I started leading the Russians to Zhang and his crew. The Rooski's now know that Matvey is being looked at by the NSA and CIA. When they figure out, or I give them the fact that Matvey is a Chinese diversion, they should start to make Zhang uncomfortable."

John was thinking, "What if the Russians just monitor Matvey?" Glenn started talking faster, "They will learn that the info Matvey has is shit;

then they will be looking for Zhang. If they do nothing then I will sick ISIS on Zhang's scary ass. In the resulting activity I will find Zhang. We will have to decide what we will do when that time comes." John was silent then, "Understood."

John changed the subject, "Tell me about Iron Wood and the park "We" built in Rockland." "We? That was all you boss; you are a charitable wonder." John slowly said, "Park and wood." Glenn knew he had nowhere to hide, "I was at war with another bidder we needed that stuff. I decided both sides had all the cash in the world so I thought outside the box, and it worked. Have we, or you, heard one ounce of noise on any device? No, and that is because of the iron wood. The only thing that was not metal that could support the weight."

John asked, "Where did the wood come from?" Glenn had talked to Nick earlier and he asked the same thing, "From Sea Captain Norlander's house just off of Jameson point in Rockland." John spoke slowly again, "Wood not house, where did the wood come from?" Glenn uneasy now, "Shhh..ah Don't have a clue." "OK so it could have been from darkest Africa shipped around the horn and crawling with demons?" "As far as I know yes"; they both lost it laughing; it was a break in the tension. Glenn was going to call Nick and find out what was going on with John.

John stood up and was walking from the kitchen to the front door, it was 6:05pm and dusk, "I still have a problem with the alarm system; I need video and thermal. I would like it throughout but right now I need it on the south side kitchen door."

John clicked his tongue twice and Molly came sleepily from the couch in the great room, "Ok let's only worry about the one that goes off all the time; can we get someone on a rocket to be here tomorrow and put this in? No, Sims is at Confidante." John opened the front door for Molly, she slowly walked out and to the edge of the front steps and sat down; her nose in the wind.

John was watching Molly closely, "Ok, give him the prepaid we use for normals. He can call me from the main gate at Sims house; I will go get him. Ok, cool, thanks; gotta go."

John sat next to Molly on her left side; she leaned into him he scratched her ears, "You let me know when they are here, ok little girl? I will do the rest." They sat there for another twenty minutes; suddenly Molly stood up looking north her nose really working; her eyes darted from what she smelled to John. John stood up; Molly got behind him and looked north from between his legs; "Good, now we know when they arrive." They went inside at 6:45pm local phantom time.

Chapter Twenty-One

5:30pm

Antwan's Diner

Rockland, Maine

After the waitress asked what he would like with his crazy old man; Nick pointed at him, "He is your father, right?" The waitress frowned, "No, Grand Father! Gonna be some tip uh mister?" Nick dropped his head, "I have been on a losing streak all day. He looked at her name tag, I am sorry Sarah; I'll have your best burger and a beer."

Nick turned to the old man as he was sitting down, "Do you remember me sir?" The old man nodded, "My name is Antwan Scales. I have been on this earth for 78 years; yes I do remember you. What took you so long?" Nick's head turned side to side like a dog listening to a whistle, "I'm sorry, what do you mean?" "I told you the house was no good that you would be sorry you bought it. Has someone died?" Nick blinked, "No, why?" "Because the black ones are killers; they will freeze your heart." Nick looked left then right; then realized he was looking for a drink. Sarah appeared as if on cue; "I thought you could use this." She set down his beer, then a shot glass of something for Antwan, and a shot of bourbon for Nick; the bourbon went first.

Nick coughed from the burn, "What are you saying?" "My great granddaddy was the one who worked on the Norlander estate since he was a young man. He was the one who found her dead." Nick holding up his hands, "Slow down I am not from around here, don't assume I know what you are talking about. Found who dead?"

Antwan threw down his shot and raised it to Sarah, "Sorry, my great granddaddy was a carpenter; he did all the work on the Norlander place. He was one of many carpenters that spent two years assembling that monster of a house. He was the one who found the captain's wife dead on the widows walk November 1875." Nick was looking at him like *more please*, "I am still lost; why is that a big deal?"

Antwan was getting frustrated; Sarah came with his drink, "Gramps tell him like you told little Mikey the first time." Antwan held up his hands like he was surrendering, "I am sorry Nick. Ruth Norlander was a devoted wife that walked her widow's walk nightly praying her husband would come home. She had called my great granddaddy Thomas, the day before she died, to check her doors.

"Thomas wanted her to contact the constable and report an attempt to break into her house. The locks and door jams were strained to the point of breaking. She said it wouldn't make any difference and sent him on his way. The next day Thomas brought the constable to the Norlander's to talk to her about her safety. That's when they found her on the walk."

Nick looked at Sarah, "Gramps tell him how she died." Antwan face flushed with embarrassment, "She was frozen. The constable said it was exposure, but Thomas said no. They both could smell death on the walk, the constable said she was beginning to turn, Thomas said no she is frozen like a block of ice. She stayed frozen in the doctor's parlor for seven days before she started to smell. The doctor said her heart was like shaved ice," Nick slammed down the rest of his beer.

Nick asked Antwan if he remembered what else he had told him three years ago. Antwan sat quietly for some seconds, "The men you stopped from buying the house had tried to buy the house many times. The captain was asked to sell it before he started the house; Thomas was afraid that there would be no work if he did; it was a big break for him.

Ruth Norlander was always complaining that these people came once a year to see if she had changed her mind. When she died she left all her money to the city to keep the house and maintain it."

Nick thought Antwan was losing time, "Antwan how can the same people try to buy the house over all this time?" He smiled, "Still think I'm crazy don't you? The same group kept trying, it was an organization of who knows what; they want that house." Nick's mind interrupted; *never reveal who the bidders were ever.*

Nick started on his burger, "Sarah can we get another round?" Antwan smiled like a little kid. Nick asked Antwan who else he should talk to about these things. Antwan, a little too relaxed, "You should go to the church and ask for the records. The pastor went insane trying to tell everyone about the danger Mrs. Norlander was in." Nick finished the second beer with his food and was a little drunk; it was way past dark.

Nick asked Sarah where he was in relation to his room at the Bed and Breakfast; she said she would call them. He thought she was nuts. "Don't you know where it is?" he hollered out while she was dialing, "I do, but you don't have to worry they have a service; they will come for you and drive your car back as well." Nick was relieved, "Wow, that is great service; old time hospitality."

She came by with the check and another beer; the check was sixty dollars. He drank his beer until the people came for him; everyone was very nice; he left three hundred dollars on the table. As he left he thanked Antwan again; Antwan was ripped and loving it.

Nick got in the courtesy car and looked back to see Sarah pick up the money. She put her hand over her mouth and her eyes welled up. Nick was a happy man; drunk happy, but actually scared shitless inside.

It was only 9:00pm and he was wasted; not good. He got the envelope out of his car before he went to his room. He ordered last minute room service; a pot of coffee and an ice cream sundae, to abate the booze. Nick liked to mix some of the coffee into the ice cream, and did so as he opened the envelope.

There were about 30 pages of information and photos, "Photos!" Nick jumped up and fired up the laptop. Glenn's stuff on the house was there; with a lot of pictures old and new.

The Norlander's house was indeed monstrous. It looked like a shaker community barn; but with beautiful doors, windows and a very long widow's walk; straight not square like at Jonesborough.

The history was a pretty dry presentation of the dates and events. Nick was surprised to learn the

Captain never returned; he was presumed lost at sea; Nick wondered considering the story he had just heard.

He went to the last page of the history and read the accounts of the groups building of the park as part of the purchase of the house. He was stacking the pages back together when a business card fell out onto the coffee table, Teshuvah LLC it had an international number.

Nick looked up the country codes; GAZA. He looked on the back to see a lipstick kiss with, "Your Competition" written in Dorothy's handwriting. Nick took another bite of ice cream, *run Stempee run!!!* He decided to call Annabel Gibson.

Nick would review all of the info he had retrieved in the morning after lots of coffee, and a good meal with Annabel. This was some scary shit, he was worried about John being alone, surrounded by these things; he called Sims.

Chapter Twenty-Two

9:00pm

Widow's Suite,

Hart Compound

John was out on the walk facing Sims' house, the phantoms were way north on the property; he thought he could use the lemonade guys to find the black ones. John needed to come up with some kind of biological names to describe the lemonade guys and the black ones, *Yes officer the lemonade one ate my friends face while the smelly black one gave me frost bite.*

John figured he had no chance of finding the black ones; the yellow guys were too far away. John's phone rang. Thank God it was Glenn, "Glenn just in time, I need your help." Glenn hesitating, "I was calling to tell you the alarm guy is on the rocket and will be there around 9:30am. Now what do you need at 9:15pm?" "Sims and I have been trying to identify some critters; they're running around at night inside the compound. I need Sims' scope, but he has it in Knoxville. Is there anything here that can do the same thing; my night spotters are one setting only?"

Glenn reminded John about the tactical night vision goggles in each of the shooting stations and three others in the storage under the rec-room. John asked, "Don't I have to charge these?" Glenn laughed, "Did you sleep through the training classes I did for everyone." "No, I was pre-occupied with getting Gavin situated at Confidante."

Glenn back on track, "Well pay attention boy, here we go; the gogs (goggles) are always charged while on station even in the stores area. They each have memory cards for recording in three modes which match Sims's scope. The run time is 16 hours with three hours of record time. You can sync them with our system and go live video through the entire system." John thanked him again, "I am going to get the gogs right now." John hung up. Glenn called Sims.

Sims answered saying, "What now?" Glenn laughed, "Down boy, what's wrong with you." "I am sitting here with Gavin and Jess drinking wine and telling rude stories about the rest of you guys." Glenn said, "Can we talk?" Sims a bit irritated, "What you too? Nick just called and said the same thing; he's worried about John at the compound."

"Well brother John is under the rec-room digging out the night vision goggles as we speak, so he can hunt down critters within the compound." Sims was trying to piece things together, "Ok I think I know what is going on. Nick has info on the critters that he doesn't want anyone to know until he verifies it. So I am going to call Nick and ream his ass and find out what he knows."

Glenn jumped in, "John and Nick have been calling me all day about the wood we got in Rockland." Sims sat up with a startled look on his face; "They want it back; Shit I got to go!" He hung up and looked at Gavin, "I got to get back to the compound." He started to go and Jess said, "I will drive I haven' been drinking remember." "Hah, the designated driver thing really works; let's go."

When they finally got in Sims' silver SUV it was 9:40pm. He pulled out his phone and called Nick. Jess was already going 80mph toward Jonesborough. He put the call on speaker and pressed the record button, "Nick, its Sims. No more bullshit, you tell me everything you know about those things running around the compound right now!" Nick sat up; he had fallen asleep for about 20 minutes; "Ok, I didn't want to tell..." Sims cut him off, "I said no bullshit, tell me what you know NOW!

Nick now just blurting things out, "These things are trouble; the black ones are killers they freeze the heart of their victims, and they smell like rotting flesh. Not sure how, but they have been part of the house since the early eighteen hundreds in Gaza; could be a lot longer. Norlander brought them to the U.S. when he bought the house.

"The people who we beat out for the sale of the wood have been trying to get their hands on it for two centuries." Sims nodding, "I shot one of their black pets dead square and it just moved on.

"Do you have a way to get together all the info on this thing?" Nick hesitated, "You get John safe and I will have all the info in thirty-six hours. I will get Glenn tracking down the other bidders; I have their card." Sims hung up and looked at Jess, "Let me tell you the story of the lemonade boys and the black holes." Sims could see the fear in her face, "Maybe I shouldn't have put that on speaker?" Jess looked at him sternly, "Ya think!"

John took Molly as far as the west kitchen doors; she would go no further. He grabbed the Mag Lite and walked across the lawn. He swept the area with his light and it was clear sailing to gravel road and then on to the rec-room.

He stopped and brought up the compound app on his phone. He turned on all the back lights including the shooting Range. The back of the property became as light as day. He turned off the mag and as he entered the rec-room. Molly was hoping to see

John again as she watched through the kitchen doors.

John turned on the lights in the stores room below and down he went. It was extremely cold down there; he scanned the area with his light. John was pretty creeped out and kept turning around as he went from box to box reading the inventory ID labels. He found the gogs and unplugged one of the units; and threw away the box. He headed back up the steps, turned out the light, closed up the rec-room and started back to the house. John killed the shooting range lights and looked for movement: nothing, they were still north he thought; he turned back on the lights; suddenly the alarm went off.

John was standing right near one of the claxon speakers; it was sudden, loud, and scared the shit out of him. He went back into the rec-room, he was moving fast now, down the steps, coded his way into the main tunnel. John checked the alarm at the stores entrance; it was the front doors. He killed the alarm, and sprinted down the tunnel and back to the house.

John came up the in kitchen. Molly was sitting in her bed looking freaked. John went to the front doors and shined his Mag lite through the glass; only the light didn't get past the glass. John stepped back; to see the entire front of the house, all of the windows and doors, were covered with black creatures. John could feel the house rumbling; the frames of the doors and windows were creaking, and starting to crack with the pressure they were applying. The wall was beginning to deform; he heard a loud snap.

Without thinking John took out his phone and lit up the entire compound. John screamed, "Take that shit; you can see that from the space station!" The rumbling stopped, and the doors and windows started to clear like someone was defrosting a windshield. In just seconds they were gone. The wall was still a little off.

John didn't notice, but he was now sitting on the floor twenty feet in front of the doors. Molly came and laid across his lap; he petted her head, "I got you little girl." He looked at his phone it was 10:45pm; it rang, it was Sims.

John answered, "Ajax liquor store." Sims smiled, "Whatta we got so far? How is your evening going?" "Me and my gal are just hanging out; sittin on the floor; counting flowers on the wall; that sorta thing; you?" Jess and I have been speedin toward Jonesborough at a hundred miles an hour; watching the stars zip by." "So you should be here any minute?" "Six, to be exact." "We'll leave the light on for ya." "Where will you guys be?" "Walking the widow; see ya soon."

Jess came up the rise heading west of Jonesborough and the sky was lit up like a there was a big stadium up ahead. Sims started laughing, "He said he would leave the light on for us." Jess laughing, "You guys are crazy." They pulled in to Sims' place and went in. He threw all of his stuff on the big couch and went back to the SUV, popped the hatch, lifted the gun compartment, took out his most prized possession, and went back.

Jess got real quiet when he came back in, "What is that?" Jess was looking at the rifle like it was a snake. Sims looked at her sternly, "Insurance." They went down to the lower level of the house and got in his golf cart. They took the tunnel to the shooting range and cut back to the rear deck. Sims showed Jess how to work the steps up to the widow's suite.

When Sims came through the door with Jess they could barely see; when their eyes adjusted to the lights they were both shaking their heads.

John was sitting on the couch and Molly was lying on her stomach with her head on John's lap. John was drinking a beer with five orange fingers. There was a bag of Cheetos by his side; Molly turned to see who was there, revealing her orange nose.

Jess looked around, "Nice and bright up here; love what you've done with the place. Sims set his rifle where he did before, retrieved two beers and he and Jess sat down. John's mouth was full, so he grunted at Sims motioning with his hand; Sims turned on the the suite's lights as John shut down the compound lighting. They could all see now.

It was quiet until Molly sneezed and wiped her nose on John's jeans. John sat forward wiped his hands on Molly's fur, motioned to Jess who got him another beer, "So, what has Nick discovered?" Sims took out his phone, looked for something, then set it down next to him, and hit play. It was the entire conversation he had with Nick as they started for Jonesborough.

When it was over John was leaning against the back door, "Shit, we need a lot of answers. We'll let Nick and Glenn do their jobs; we've got to figure these things out." Sims cut in, "Varmints; vermin." John raised his right arm in victory, "Great names! We got to kick some vermin ass." John sat nodding, still glad they had something to call them, "Get some sleep we will start in the morning. There is a diner west of here I've wanted to try. Say 6:00am?"

John asked Jess if she had an overnight bag. She had thrown one in the SUV while Sims was putting his arsenal in the gun compartment. John nodded, he was starting to crash; the beer was over taking the adrenalin. He went out on the east walk, he couldn't see anything; he half smiled thinking that's a little better; then the smile went away, *what if only the black ones are out there right now?*

Chapter Twenty- Three

Day Three

6:00am

Bed and Breakfast

Rockland, Maine

Nick carried his crowded plate down the breakfast buffet, and then refilled his coffee mug and carafe. He sat at a corner table and waited. When he called Annabel Gibson late last night she was just getting into bed. He introduced himself and asked her to meet him for breakfast.

She was reluctant; Nick offered her five hundred dollars to eat a free breakfast and listen to his problem. He knew when she mentioned the money to her husband she would be joining him. Nick gave her his number and a cursory explanation of his problem so she could think on it.

Annabel was a tall lady, mid-forties, of slender build, with reddish light brown hair and hazel eyes. She dressed like someone who was trying not to look like they lived in Rockland. He saw her looking around and waved; she came over. He stood they introduced themselves and he poured her some coffee. When she got her coffee just right, Nick handed her an envelope with five hundred dollars inside. She looked inside and smiled, "What can I do for you Mr. Hart?"

Nick swallowed his food, took a sip of coffee, and wiped his mouth, "I need to know everything there is to know about the Norlander house and all the lore that goes with it. Just so you know, I had dinner with Antwan Scales last night and I was given this by Dorothy Wickem." He handed her the card; he had not anticipated her turning it over. She smiled, is that why you called so late Mr.Hart?" Nick now beet red, "Ah, no; I was asking Antwan the same questions ten different ways, trying to get one clear answer." He handed her the folded piece of paper; she raised her brows and said nothing.

Nick started over, "Do you know Antwan's tale of the death of Ruth Norlander?" Annabel shifted in her seat, "Yes I do and I believe that he believes it without question." Nick looked at her, "Gibby is it?" She nodded, "I need to know if you can do this work without being bias against any information you come across, and present it all in good faith; regardless how bizarre you may find it. At this point one tiny bit of information you deem unimportant could cost someone their life. Can you do that?"

She was becoming very uncomfortable, "I can, but I am not sure I want to. Digging into this stuff could ruin my reputation; I am not a researcher of spooky tales Mr. Hart. My reputation has been built by studying the real peoples of the upper Atlantic Coast. Their story; how these peoples from all over the world combined all of their histories together. How they survived to create micro-cultures all up and down the region. Real, historic, everyday people; not myths and ghosts Mr. Hart.

"Well Gibby I am not a teller of spooky tales that needs some weird ass stuff dug up to amuse myself. There are some realities that are kicking my ass right now and I need your help to defend the people I love.

"What I am is someone who is offering you two hundred fifty thousand dollars to get every last piece of information you can find on the Norlanders; what killed them; who has been trying to buy that house since 1872; and you will only have 36 hours to get this done.

"Now you cannot tell anyone about this. I Know Dorothy and her pals will want to know what happened with her recommendation and gossip blah blah; but you will have to be completely professional in this case. That's why I am paying this kind of money. Also, if you feel info is dubious then note that but include it. So whatta ya say Gibby?"

At this point Gibby was staring into space; Nick guessed that she had not heard a word after he mentioned the money. She finally came back and said, "I will have to pay for various things and favors, including secrecy." Nick smiled, "I need as much documentation as possible; buy original documents if need be, offer stupid sums of money just get them if you can.

"My group has unlimited resources and can determine many things from original documents; are we clear?" Nick was hoping Gibby's efforts would attract Tashuvah LLC and force them to contact him.

She was in shock but her mind was racing, "I will need cash." Nick smiled, "You are asking the right kinds of questions." He handed her another envelope; inside she saw an ATM card and two credit cards; one of them was black and made of metal. He gave her a business card, "Use this bank and show them this card; they will take care of what you need." Nick was curious to see if that information got back to Tashuvah as well.

"According to Antwan the best place to start is in the basement of the church where the Norlanders attended back in the day. If your husband has any problems with this I can arrange a holiday for him; you know an all-expenses paid trip to get the hell out of our way." She laughed; that was a good sign.

Chapter Twenty-Four

6:00am

Breakfast

West of Jonesborough

At 5:45 they were all climbing into Sims' SUV; Sims was at the wheel, Jess riding shotgun, with Molly and John in the back. Molly was sitting at attention trying to figure out where they were going.

Sims turned to John, "Where to?" John winked and nodded at Molly. He told Sims to turn on the voice for the NAV; he did so. John smiling and looking at Molly, "Coffee west of Jonesborough"; Molly got excited spinning in place trying to lick John's face. Jess was laughing, "She must really like her coffee." "No she is just hoping to get pieces of my donut." Sims looked in the rear view, "Thought we were going to a diner?" "It's across the street from the Coffee Hole, our early morning hang out."

Sims, NAV didn't want to take the same route as John's; he was surprised, "Sims you put this same unit in my Polaris didn't you?" "Yup, why?" John just shook his head and pointed out the turn just in time. Having found the road, they turned right into the sleepy little town. They parked down a ways because Sammy's Diner was crowded; there were twelve people in there and it looked like they may have to wait.

As they entered and looked around they noticed the diner had three booths on each side forming an aisle to a counter that appeared to be just short of the width of the diner. As you entered further you could see an entry to a side room with ten tables. It was perfectly empty for what John had planned.

John stood at the entry waiting for a waitress to seat them then it hit him, *what, you think you are the emperor you can't seat yourself*; he went back and they sat at a table in the front left corner by the windows. They had been sitting for about three minutes when he noticed no one was even looking at them; he got up and stood by the counter.

Finally, an older waitress asked what he wanted. John turned and pointed, "We have been sitting in there for about five minutes and no one has come to help us." The waitress kept moving while saying, "Ain't nobody gonna help you in there today; everybody knows that room is only open on Saturdays and Sundays." John stood there with his mouth hanging open.

He looked up and saw an older man cooking in the back; he turned to look at John his apron had his name on it, "Sammy." Sammy turned away trying to avoid him.

John took his wallet out and held up two one hundred dollar bills and waved them at Sammy. Sammy acting pissed stopped what he was doing and came around to the front, "What do you want mister?" John doing a dumb new neighbor routine, "I am new to this town and have been getting my morning coffee across the street at 4:00am; Phu and Adam told me to try the diner that it was very good." Sammy stood taller, "It is, so what do you want?"

John tired of the whole mess, "Look I came here to have some breakfast and a meeting with my associates and I am told you only open the side room on the weekend." "That's right, so?" So I want to rent the room for one hundred dollars an hour and we will still pay for our breakfast. That ain't breakin the rules is it?" Sammy was looking at the money, "No we do catering as well." John stepped in on Sammy and got close enough to freak him out, "If this works out I may be renting that side room a lot; do you have blinds or curtains for it?" Sammy's eyes were real big now, "You call ahead and we'll make it more private." John slipped the money in his hand, "Now can I get my coffee? I really need some coffee."

The coffee was as good as Phu's, the food was as country good as it gets, and the mean ol' lady was real nice now. Sims bet John fifty bucks she was Sammy's wife. Jess scolded them both; John took the bet.

When they finished their food, Sims got up and went out to the SUV; Jess said, "Where is he going?" John leaned back in his chair, "He is going to see his girlfriend." Jess's eyes darted for a mico second and John crossed his arms, *Jess likes Sims; Jess likes Sims.* Sims put on Molly's leash; they were heading for Phu's vacant lot. The ol' waitress came in and saw what they were looking at, "Does she go inside with you at the Hole?" John turned and looked at her, "Yes Phu approves of Molly so far." That's good enough for us." John was shocked for two reasons first he owed Sims fifty bucks and there were health laws to consider, "Won't you get cited for health violations?" "Shit honey you are up in the trees now; don't worry about that."

John got out fifty bucks and set it next to Sims coffee cup. Jess looked at it then back to John, "How do you know you lost the bet?" "I only mentioned Phu to Sammy."

Sims put Molly back in the SUV then leaned in and pointed to his left shirt pocket; she moved in very slowly and with her lightest touch used her front teeth and carefully pulled out a napkin filled with bacon. Sims patted her on the head and came back into the diner.

Everyone was smiling at him like he was a celebrity. He sat down put his fifty bucks away without saying a word; he waved to the ol'gal and she topped off his coffee. He looked at John, "Words out, you are the new rich guy in town; women will come callin."

It was 7:30 and John needed to get it going, "Sims and I have to be back by 9:00 the alarm guy is coming. Ok what do we know?" Sims started, "Nick is finding out everything he can about the wood and the vermin that were haunting the Norlanders. What he does know is freaky; I thought what we were messing with the other night was harmless; now not so much."

John leaned in, "Last night they showed they are intelligent and can plan on the fly." Sims looked worried and leaned back, "How so?" "Well they had planned to take the kitchen door on again; but I lit up the back so much they couldn't do anything without being seen, or they just can't do light. That caused them to change plans and come at us from the front."

Jess asked, "All the varmints move together right so could the yellow ones do the door in the light?" John started to answer, "The yellow ones…were not there last night; they stayed way to the north. Only the black ones were involved last night; they went somewhere after I hit the full compound button on the light app."

He looked at Sims, "You said you thought the one you shot turned into smoke?" Sims looked right; he was visualizing, "It dissolved, then like blew away; but slowly." John said, "Last night when I hit them with the all the lights it was like someone defrosted a windshield." Sims was nodding, "Yup same deal."

Jess was confused, "Why does that help." "They change shape, they have density if they can push on the doors to set off the alarm they might be able to grab someone like Nick was saying." Jess sat back, "Well shit then they are actually living creatures?" Sims said, "In Afghanistan the tribesmen would say they are spirits; essence of things once living."

Jess shaking her head, "You guys are totally off the rails here don't ya think?" She got up and went to the ladies room. John turned to Sims, "You scared the piss out of her; a little heavy with the spirits thing?" Sims looked John in the eye, "I wasn't kidding."

Sims sat back again, "Maybe the yellow bastards are the planners and the black vermin are the soldiers.

John looked around to see if Jess was coming back, "I didn't want to tell you this with Jess around; last night those suckers were determined to get in the house. They pressed against the entire front of the house; must have been a hundred of them trying to break through the walls and doors.

The whole house was shaking and rumbling the jams and sills were cracking before I hit the lights. If they can crush the front of a house they should have no problem smashing our asses."

Sims' a little wide eyed, I'll call Confidante and have them arrange a car for her." John nodded, "Good." *Yellow bastards, and the black vermin; names are getting better.* "Maybe tonight we can determine how they move and work together." Sims nodded.

Chapter Twenty-Five

9:00am

Jameson Point

Rockland, Maine

Gibby left breakfast went home and got her husband on board; she told him everything; including keeping everything quiet. With his blessing, she headed to the bank; she withdrew ten thousand dollars which she thought was a ridiculous amount.

She headed for the church to see Pastor Todd Luedtke over by Jameson Point. When she arrived she went around the south side of the building to the rectory. She found Todd at his desk, "Pastor Luedtke, I was wondering if I could take some of your time? I need your help; I have a client that is in dire need of information I think you may have in your basement records.

Luedtke stood and shook her hand, "I don't have a lot just the old registries and personal stuff documenting all the Luedtke Pastors who have headed this church; going back to 1862."

Gibby smiled, "That is precisely why I am here; your great great grandfather was the Norlander's pastor in 1875 isn't that correct?" Todd held up his hands, "I have no idea. I don't see the good in going backwards, we should be ever moving forwards don't you agree?" Gibby did actually, "Yes I do, but my client feels that certain peoples' futures hang in the balance and I must get what I can to help him.

"He is willing to pay to look at them or pay a nice sum to own them." Luedtke was looking down at his feet then to Gibby back and forth, "Let's go look at what we have; I have not been down there since I was a kid. We are still working with my father's registry, and there isn't extra anything left to store now days."

She followed Luedtke around to the back of the church to what looked like doors going down to a root cellar. He opened them and looked inside; He stepped through the spider webs to a light switch; the light came on. Todd turned to Gibby, "Who said miracles have passed away; give me a second and I will clear the way." She was getting excited; she loved hunting down obscure information; gems she knew that everyone had forgotten. Leudtke emerged with a broom sweeping away dust and webs, "Now give this a minute and we should be able to breathe down there."

Leudtke led the way. He came to another switch he hadn't seen and turned it on; the whole area came alive. There were three rows on old metal shelves; four shelves to each section and three sections to a row; all filled with dusty boxes and bins. Everything was in boxes; nothing lying loose.

Gibby smiled, "Looks like someone took the time to protect what was down here; maybe we can actually use some of this. How do you want to do this?"

Leudtke surprised Gibby, "Give me a price for the whole lot, less the registries or anything else obvious to church business. You arrange to haul it out and clean the space when you are done." Gibby was very happy, "I will make a call, and then I will make you an offer. Pastor Leudtke what do you make in a year?" He looked down at the floor, "Nine thousand, plus the offering; all the maintenance is voluntary or it does not get done." She smiled then turned away, *Jesus that sucks, shouldn't your boys make more than that?*

She called Nick who was not too happy to hear from her; "Are you stuck?" Gibby was taken back, "Just wanted to tell you the pastor will let me buy everything for one price; this guy only makes nine grand a year!" "Gibby I don't really know why you have called. I told you to pay ridiculous amounts for what we want; let me give you an example, and then you won't have to call me every five minutes. Pay the pastor thirty thousand for the junk and have it moved to a place you can work with it. You need a moving company that is going broke and a store front you can rent to do the rest of the work. Now go and do your job." Nick hung up. Gibby turned back to Todd, "You are in luck Pastor Leudtke."

Chapter Twenty-Six

10:15am

Hart Compound

John and Sims had just finished with the alarm contractor; they showed him the area assured him they knew all of this was overkill and now he was busy. They had to wait around until he was done so they could verify everything was the way they wanted it. They had parked in the great room with Molly on the throw rug, Sims in a recliner and John had his feet up while on the couch.

They were discussing strategy concerning Glenn. He was trying to nail down Zhang while building a 3D image of the Norlander place using the matching info from the photos. Now they had added a language search so they could read the markings. They felt the less he was involved in their pest control the better.

Sims suggested that Glenn devise a way to get overhead thermal images from the satellites; General Rouse be damned. John said he had to think on that one.

They were both about to suggest checking up on the alarm guy when the seventy-six inch monitor on the south wall lit up. Sims and John stood up and started moving toward it; Sims went to the right of the screen and flipped the light switch and a key board was added below the screen.

The screen was set up in a 4 up configuration with two of the top boxes having what looked like weather charts and the bottoms were static at the moment.

The sender was Glenn. Before John could say anything Glenn started talking in his best Monty Python English accent, "Message for you sir!" John looked at Sims who was smiling. John, Nick and Glenn had spent a large part of their youth in various stages of mental enhancement watching the old comedy greats like Monty Python, Faulty Towers, Hudson and Landry, In Living Color, Mel Brooks and Oliver Stone. Sims had learned to love the stuff watching the three of them needle each other; Glenn had just activated a skit from Monty Python (youtube Monty Python - Message for you sir).

John kept it going, "Message you say?" "Yes" "Well go on then" "We have a problem Sir." "Problem you say" "Yes Sir, a small problem actually; about the size of your wee Sir." "My wee?" "Yes Sir." Sims could tell that Glenn and John could not keep it up much longer without losing it. "Well let's see it man." The monitor loaded the bottom two boxes. "Are you seeing the charts Sir" "Why yes I can; I can also see why you spoke of my wee." Glenn had not expected John to rebound; he should have been laughing way to hard by now; "Why is that Sir" "It's obvious enough to see why; the cold front is two hundred yards wide." Sims fell out laughing; John followed. Glenn, back in Colorado, was shaking his head with tears running down his face. It took them a couple of minutes to focus again and talk trash back and forth.

John looked closer, "Why do we care about a cold front way up on Canada's border?" Glenn pointed out the small warm front coming up towards shore in the Gulf. "John, can you make out the path of each storm?" John baffled, "Again, what the hell?" Glenn knew he had him when he heard the frustration in his voice. "Well, let me enhance if for you kid." The lower left screen now presented both storms and showed a line connecting the two. Somewhat more subdued John slowly said, "Are you saying that these tiny storms are going to somehow survive to join up?"

"I am not saying that exactly. I am just trying to point some things out; like the National Weather Services hasn't even picked up on the fact that both storms are on the same track and adjusting speeds. If one speeds up, the other one slows. The opposite is also true.

"Now, if they do continue at their current speed and tracks…" Glenn stopped speaking and dropped the bomb. John looked as the lower right box was now showing the blinking yellow light flashing on John's house. Glenn, back to his English accent added, "Just saying' sir. I am glad I took notice of this. If we had waited for an actual report we could have been caught with our knickers down." John looked at Sims; they both were thinking the same bad thoughts.

John didn't answer. He was staring at the blinking light. No longer in a playful mood, "Zoom in and show the house Google style." The screen changed and all four video boxes blended into one big screen. The image now filed half of the wall. It zoomed down towards the earth following the yellow dot. It went through the dot and stopped about a hundred feet above John's house. The view was from the front angle.

"Now lay in the path line and yellow indicator." The picture changed again. The line cut the house right down the middle. Not kind of in the middle, but perfectly in half. The blinking light was at the front door as though it was about to ring the bell.

John walked to the wall and typed in his code and pushed a couple of keys the maps and charts were replaced by a full wall image of Glenn. John just looked at him for a few moments, waiting for a reaction. Glenn was a funny guy, but he had a bullshit meter, and it was flashing. John finally broke the silence, "So, is anything you showed me true or have you spent the last fifteen minutes yanking my chain?" Glenn, unmoved, "Well, all of the information is true, but I did present it so as to prey upon your tornado phobia." John's eyes widened, "Phobia? You were there! That was some real shit Glenn!" Glenn lowered his head as if he had been shamed and said, "God this is fun." John threw up both hands and said, "Is there anything to this?"

John walked over next to Sims who was still glum, "Well, these storms have beaten the odds for the last two days, and that is the real reason I called. We should have a plan." John sat down in one of the chairs and put his elbows on his knees and his head in his hands. Molly was lying on her back looking at him upside down.

When he looked up, Glenn was looking at him concerned. "I don't like it when you do that. What kind of problem are you thinking we have? John looked at Glenn. "We need you here; it is 11:30am, see you for dinner; we'll arrange pick-up. Glenn started to say something, but was cut off when John ended the call.

John looked at Sims; Sims was staring at the front doors imagining the black vermin outside, raised his eye brows, "Sauron covered the sun so the Orks could move during the day." "That, with a little Ghost busters; is that what we're looking at?"

Sims looked back where the monitor was, "Tonight is going to be big we've got to figure this shit out. I will call and make arrangements for Glenn."

John stood up and laughed, "God I am glad I am not having dreams for at least three more days." Sims gave him a half hug, "Me too man, me too." John went to check on the alarm guy.

Glenn stared at the blank screen; he wondered why John had changed so fast and was so worried. He started to get pissed; someone was keeping him in the dark.

One of his computers chimed; it had completed its task. He was waiting for the report to print, but nothing happened. He went to check on the results and there was only one word, "Aramaic." The only note was a footnote, "No translations available." Glenn went on Google and put in Aramaic and it came back as an ancient language that died out about the time Jesus was killed. So, Aramaic was popular before Jesus not so much after; overtaken by Hebrew and Greek. Glenn ran the history through his mind; it seemed to make sense, *so why the hell was it carved into his wood, in his compound? Was the house built that long ago?*

Glenn had a plane to catch; he picked up his go bag and went. He would work in shooting station 3 or the main track under the great room; depending on what John wanted. All he knew was someone owed him some information and an apology.

He called Jess from the shuttle; he knew he could get her talking. She picked up and they both said hello, then he said, "Geez pretty wild times at the compound aye?" She let it go. He smiled as she unloaded; when he hung up he was no longer smiling*; damn!*

It had taken the alarm guy three hours, but he had it working. Sims and John took turns learning how to use and adjust the new software and how to reposition the lens. They heated up their arms with hot water and the sensors picked up a three degree change either way colder or hotter; very impressive. It had zoom so you could move in tight on door knob or take it back to a wide angle to see the entire entry. John made sure it could be viewed from every security panel in the compound. He thought he should have done this long before now; *before now there were no vermin.*

Chapter Twenty-Seven

12:30pm

Rockland, Maine

Gibby had done as Nick had suggested and gathered all the stuff from the basement into the back dining hall of the local American Legion. Three thousand dollars got her two days no questions and no personnel on site.

She had called the local high school and enticed a coach into sending over the boys' basketball team; she offered fifteen hundred dollars for new uniforms. The boys set up eight large folding tables in two columns and four rows. They then put the boxes and bins neatly under the tables.

She arranged for the girl's team to arrive thirty minutes after the boys had left; she provided them with twenty-five hundred dollars for uniforms and sweat suits. She gave the girls a pile of yard sticks and told them to carefully empty each box or bin on the table above where it sat and isolate it with a yard stick.

Soon there was complete order where bedlam had been. They hadn't needed all eight tables; which left her two for isolating the priorities. The entire effort had taken four hours; she had thirty hours more to go.

Todd Luedtke remembered that there was a church safety deposit box. He was grateful for the money and the cleanup job the scouts and done; so he wanted to bring the contents of it to Gibby. Luedtke called to find out where she wanted him to deliver it.

She was now trying to figure how much time she had to sort and if she could sort and read in time; she needed help. Maybe the pastor would stay; he knew the obscure names in the various families; she could hope.

When Luedtke arrived she was waiting outside; Luedtke was carrying a shopping bag; they went into the dining hall. Luedtke was slowly looking from table to table, "I didn't think there was this much stuff down there."

Gibby was glad he seemed curious, "Well it is organized I just have to go through it." Todd nodded not taking the bait, "Well let's see what is in here." He put the bag on the last table on the right and stepped away, "Well take a look" he was motioning to Gibby.

She looked inside then poured the contents on the table; a small key went bouncing across the floor; Todd retrieved it for her. In the middle of the pile was what looked like an old journal; it looked like it was made for a man; it had a lock.

There were several documents folded so they would fit in the deposit box. Gibby still looking at the pile, "Was this just stuffed in the deposit box?" Todd nodded, "The clerk pressed down while I turned the key and it popped open; I put the bag over the box then we turned it so everything had to fall in the bag; that's all of it."

Gibby looked at the folded papers they appeared to be hand sketched maps of movements or path ways. She moved on; there were ten letters from Ruth Norlander to her husband; all sealed no postage. She found Leudtke father's will and a note explaining the journal and the drawings as his great, great grandfather's most protected items; "His obsessions." Gibby was thinking, *jack pot!*

Gibby looked up at Todd, "Wow this is some really good stuff; your great great grandfather was the Norlander's pastor; will you stay and help me get through the rest of this stuff? There might be a lot more to learn about your family history."

Leudtke was fixated on the tables, he walked through them one more time, "This all belongs to you now; I have to get back to the church. I just wanted to see if there was anything important related to current or future church business." Gibby absently said, "Always moving forward right pastor?" Leudtke raised a hand and waved; and kept on walking to his car.

Gibby opened the diary and read the first page; she just kept staring at it. In somewhat of a daze she went to the first row of tables Leudtke's great great grandfather's journal was actually the history of the legendary aberrations of Jameson point; he had mentioned Ruth keeping the same type of journal to ensure that one of the journals would survive. *Could Antwan, Ruth and Luedtke all have been loopy?*

She was now on a mission to find Ruth's journal; if it existed. She looked under the tables reading what was written on each of the empty boxes; a plastic bin had a faded NORL showing with the rest of the name unreadable. She stepped up to the table and started to look.

The girl who worked this box was obviously a slob; she just made a big pile and left. Gibby started to move a couple of the items and the whole pile fell off the back of the table; spilling in every direction on the floor. She stood there stunned with a doily in her hand.

She went around to the back of the table; there was what looked like an ancient music box. She moved all the other debris, and then picked it up; it was quite heavy. Gibby made her way to the uncluttered back table and set it down. She opened the box to find another journal, it was made for a women; no key required. She read the first two pages then called Nick. Nick answered and asked her to wait.

Nick was just finishing the work on the company cars with Gavin. Gavin had said he was getting really worried about the guys at the compound because of what was there. Nick asked him how he knew about all of this; apparently Jess had come straight to him when she returned from driving Sims to Jonesborough.

Nick kind of lost his mind, "Damn it; please get Jess in line and tell her to keep her wits about her, and stop talking. I just hope Glenn hasn't called her." Gavin sighed, "Too late she told me all about Glenn's reaction when she told him everything. Did you know Sims shot one of these things and it didn't die?"

Nick really frustrated, "Look we are working that end we have several things going that will render the situation; so you and Jess keep things together and get more invisible every damn day.

Right now this Zhang asshole is your biggest problem. Glenn is zeroing in on Zhang's location; your job is not to do anything to draw attention to yourselves. He can't find the lower levels" Gavin not known for sarcasm, "You mean our collider mesh and a thousand percent increase in antenna gain. Hope Zhang doesn't find that shit?" Nick now at ropes end, "Damn straight Skippy." He hung up.

He picked up Gibby, "Thanks for waiting; what do you have for me?"Gibby relayed all the info regarding the diaries; and their records that spanned over three years.

Each had detailed accounts of encounters with the aberrations. She felt it would be better if he could personally get these to his people and they could be working on them while she went through the rest of the piles. Nick agreed and said he would come and pick it up.

Nick called John; it was 3:30pm. John picked up, "Nick how goes the search?" "Our girl hit pay dirt; found the journals of Ruth Norlander and her pastor, a guy named Luedtke. Both journals were written in parallel to ensure one journal would survive; they both survived and we have them.

I need a private plane courier nonstop to you guys; maybe one of your gun makers on this coast. Have him call me on a burner when he arrives; I will meet him.

You guys need to have this right away; there will be a lot of lore to go through. Our girl will keep working on this end; these results came much quicker than I expected; let's take advantage."

John was starting to feel the stress, "Good work we'll make sure to jump right on this stuff. Any ripples from the Teshuvah boys?" "Not yet, but while there is the appearance of a secret being kept; we are leaving a trail Helen Keller could follow; won't be long. I gotta go get these things and lock'em up." Nick grabbed his keys and headed for the American Legion Hall

Chapter Twenty-Eight

3:55pm

Hart Compound

John called Molly and they went for a walk in the front of the property. Molly was sniffing and he was thinking; all these strange events piled into the last couple of days like something big was building. He needed an estimate on the storm's arrival time.

Everything seemed to be about two days away; if that. Molly's leash went taut and broke his focus; Molly had stopped she was staring at something in the furthest most corner of the lot; right behind Sims' house, but on John's side of the fence.

They both stayed perfectly still; John was trying to see exactly what she smelled, then he saw it; amongst all the shadows of the tall foliage was the faintest shadow of a man; almost like a paper cutout.

John moved slowly toward Molly, "Molly ready," she sat at attention her whole upper body leaning into her target; she was softly whining, he removed her leash, "Molly go!" She took off like an arrow dead on target. He looked hard to see the shadow again but couldn't make it out.

John was racing to stay within sixty yards of her. When she arrived at her target she started working the ground; smelling for the intruder. She was looking at the top of the foliage barking; she was really breathing hard; intent on getting her teeth into something. John put her leash back on and gave it a tug; she sat down. She was still focused on where she thought he went up and over the fence.

John grabbed his phone he pushed one button, Sims said, "Yes." John calmly, "bogey your northwest corner on the move; Molly had him; grey on grey shadow suit; no status." "Roger that; Sims out." John took off her leash again, "Sims' go" She ran along the side of the fence to its opening; she went through and back to Sims' on the other side. As she made the turn to go back John heard Sims fire his rifle; he knew that sound; he immediately started thinking of how they would process the body; Sims didn't miss.

Sims and Molly came through the fence opening in his cart. They picked up John and headed back to Sims'. Molly was now on John's lap and was breathing normally; John scratched her ears, "Nice catch Molly; your nose is much better than my eyes."

John looked at Sims, "Well?" "He looks Middle Eastern, but not like the afghan boys." "So we can get a good photo?" "Yup; in the right ear out the back; face intact." John sighed, "You got all you need down here, or do we need to go back up?" Sims stopping the cart at the entrance to his trash area, "I got what we need; a full murder kit on this guy right?" John nodded.

John followed Sims into the trash area where his two barrels had been knocked over with a body sandwiched in between. John took a look at everything, "How did you get to him so fast?" Sims pointed at his SUV; "I just got my rifle out of the back and was gonna put it the cart with some other stuff for tonight and you called. I took off the safety and moved toward the corner and this ninja looking asshole was walking the fence like a cat; he had no chance. Do we call General Rouse, or we gonna mention this to him later?"

John looked at his watch, 5:20pm, "Who is your courier for Nick?" Sims was trying to get one of the trash barrels out of the way, "Marko from Jersey." "Good, he is from Nick's part of the woods. So Marko can swing over the Atlantic and then deliver the murder kit for Nick to process?" "I will ask him when he gets here; we will have to bag this guy and load him for Marko." John agreed, "Let's make sure Marko is compensated for his emotional damages.

He will have to pay a friend to help him drop the ninja in the Atlantic."

It took them another hour to process the kit for Nick, bag his clothes for Glenn, and get him ready for Marko. Marko waved to Glenn on his way out, as Glenn pulled in, "I am starving what's for dinner?" Sims looked at John, "Coffee west of Jonesborough?" John was about to agree, when he was rammed by Molly; she agreed.

John and Molly road with Glenn up to the house, while Sims cleaned up and put together all the stuff he would need for the night. He packed 4 phosphorous grenades, *you hate light? You gonna love these.*

Sims called Nick, "Nick, we had our first ripple. The problem is they knew to come here; they had a guy in the compound." Nick was quiet for a second, "We know it is not the phones; did John go into Jonesborough lately?" Sims sighed, "No but I went to Confidante, and when I got back John had the whole place lit up like the sun. I think they think I am the head of house."

Nick added, "While Glenn is there have him make sure who ever it was didn't leave anything behind. Have him check all our wireless shit for fleas."

While they were driving to the diner, John and Sims were talking like Glenn had been there all day; they kept watching his face get a more and more worried look. Sims looked in the rear view at John, "You gonna rent the side room in case Glenn starts screaming?" John smiled at Sims, "We gotta hurry Sammy closes at 8:00pm.

Chapter Twenty-Nine

6:00pm

American Legion Hall

Rockland, Maine

.

Nick arrived at the American Legion Hall and was met out front by Gibby; she had the journals in her purse. She started to show them to Nick, "Not out here please; let's get inside." She took him to the dining hall; he immediately started walking up and down the rows of stuff. Nick went to the back tables and looked at what Gibby had been setting a side.

He was about to move on to the journals, when something caught his eye; it was half of a drawing sticking out from under a stack of seemingly meaningless pages. He pulled it out and held it up to the light; it was opaque, possibly parchment. It looked like a detailed drawing of the timber frame Norlander house. All of the pieces were there with the numbers showing the connection points; like 1:1 would be a match and 2:2 and so on.

He looked in the lower right hand corner and there was a legend; there were names that went with each match. The title of the legend corresponded with the carvings over the mantle that was now the south kitchen door of the compound. Under the script was a translation; "Abbadon Shall Lead Us"; then there was a script followed by 9:1-11. There was no translation for the script before the numbers.

Nick looked stunned and confused; Gibby was looking at him with a knowing look, "Pretty wild stuff don't you agree?" He mumbled, "Especially if what's his name's front door is now your kitchen door." She couldn't make out what he was saying, "Well take a look at these." She handed him the journals. He opened Ruth's journal first. He leafed through several pages while shaking his head, it was like his mind was saying no, no, no.

He picked up Luedtke's journal and did the same flipping back and forth; suddenly he flipped back and stood completely still staring at the page he was on. He could not make his brain accept what he was seeing; it was a miniature of the same drawing he had been looking at except it was labeled differently. The legend was the same but there was a subtitle; The Major Demons of Hell; each demon had a matching number preceding the name. This was a ranking of the worst hell had to offer and each had a connection named after them; or they were the place holder of that intersection. He went back to the table and grabbed the first drawing; all the names matched the locations and the legend. Nick looked back at the script on the mantle it had a translation it read Revelations 9:1-11.

Nick went back to the pile of papers he thought were meaningless; now he was making some sense out of some of them. He found an old five and dime style composition book and he leafed through it; it was an attempt to describe the jobs of all the demons and their relationships to the others.

When he got past the demon section he saw a heading that said, "Teshuvah". Nick was now blinking rapidly trying to deflect all he was forced to absorb. Under the heading was a subheading, The Agents of Abbadon. It outlined the activity of the group and their attempts to buy the Norlander house from the Captain in Gaza in 1860. They tried again in the United States at Rockland on three different occasions ending in spring 1875 each time the suitor was named Semjaza.

Nick was pacing up and down the rows when his burner phone rang, "Hello?" "Mr. Nick I have a delivery for you, where do you want to meet." Nick gave him the address to the bed and breakfast.

Nick looked at Gibby, "This is great work, now find all that is related to these six items and box them for shipping right away; then call me." Nick left with the journals and the composition book; his mind was so overwhelmed, he almost crashed three times on the way back to his room.

Marko was waiting in the bar adjoined to the B&B. Marko was an Italian with long jet black hair, worn in a small pony tail. He was right at six feet tall; he had a thin chin strap beard.

Nick sat down and ordered a drink, "What are you drinking" Marko looked at his glass, "Sparkling water, John said to stay ready; you might have something coming back." Nick smiled, "You got GPS?" "Don't need it; I lived here for six years back in the day." "You ever hear of the ghosts on Jameson Point?" Marko stood up, took the journals and book, "They're why we left; bad shit; on my way back." Nick slid him an envelope, "Do you need one for your friend?" Marko waved it off and left; headed for the American Legion Hall. Now Nick was a complete mess. He called John.

Chapter Thirty

7:25pm

Sammy's Diner

West of Jonesborough

As Sims pulled into a spot in front of the diner; John's phone rang, "Nick, whatta you got?" John was listening as he walked into the diner; Sammy smiled and looked at the clock; John held up four fingers, and then held up four fingers again, followed by two fingers; Sammy seemed much happier. He joined Sims and Glenn in their usual corner; John smiled to see the ol' gal was petting Molly. Nick finished his tale of Teshuvah and Semjaza and John hung up.

When the ol' gal finished petting Molly John slipped her the four hundred dollars, "Now, I won't get in trouble with Sammy if I give this to you will I?" She laughed, "I'm gonna get it from him anyway." Sims was smiling at John; John just shook his head.

Glenn on edge a bit, "What did Nick have to say?" "He said he has a lot of work for you; he found some notes, both journals and the translations for all the carvings on the wood." Glenn was getting into it now, "So what did it say?" "Well Glenn you got to help us with that."

Glenn finally was fed up with John and Sims treating him like a kid, "Ok what the hell is going on; you guys have been on my ass for no reason since yesterday?" John looked him in the eye, "How did your chat with Jess go?" Glenn looked down, "Well no one was telling me anything and I was getting pissed." John leaned back in his chair, "So you decided Jess should get her ass chewed because you couldn't trust us to tell you what you thought you should know?" "What?"

John very quiet now, "Jess is a total geek; not a geek like us now, but like we used to be. We need her brain intact, not stressed; she is going to have her own company in two months, and she wants to build a new company from another of her ideas; outside of the cellular world. I told her I would back her if she needed it. So in just a few hours we have managed to fry her circuits."

John saw Sammy's wife coming with plates of food thrown together family style, "Here, you guys look hungry so Sammy put on little of everything we were serving today so you could eat what you want when you want." Sims got a big smile on his face as

Sammy came in with a cooler on wheels and a raw plate for Molly. He even had green bottles of sparkling water, and of course, plenty of beer. Sammy handed John a key in an envelope, "Lock up and give this to Phu when you leave, he starts work over there in about fifteen minutes." He and the wife left. John, Sims and Glenn sat there stunned; Glenn finally said, "Never see that shit in California." John gave everyone a beer and they toasted Sammy and the wife. Sims mentioned they should find out her name. John smiled, "Its Bev."

They ate and drank while John and Sims took turns getting Glenn up to speed. Glenn started to give them the latest on Zhang when John raised his hand; he looked at Sims, "Take Glenn and sweep the place; after Glenn found transmitters in the Ninja's pajamas we take nothing for granted." While they did the sweep, John put the leftovers in the fridge and cleaned up their table.

The place was cleared; Sims leaned to John while he was walking by, "Nick wanted to know if you went into town while I was in Knoxville?" John cringed, "Shit! Follow the stranger; damn." Then Glenn took all the time he needed to really explain who Zhang was and how he operated.

John looked at his watch; it was quickly heading towards 9:00pm. Glenn wondered, "It's been dark awhile will they be out running around when we get there?" John moving with Molly toward the front door, "Sims you lock up, I will water Molly and Glenn you get on your laptop and check to see if they are waiting for us in the kitchen." Sims trotted over to the Coffee Hole, introduced himself to Phu, and gave him the key.

John came back with Molly and everyone loaded into Sims' SUV. As they started back, Sims activated his hands free, "Call Allison" it went to work; Marko's voice came through the speakers; "Allison is not home yet, she should be back by 9:30 would you like to leave a message?" "Yes, please tell Allison to always drive with her brights on in the dark." "Thank you I will tell her. Goodbye."

Glenn turned to John, "Nobody in the kitchen yet, but look at this." John moved Molly so he could look over Glenn's shoulder, "What am I looking at?" Glenn went to full screen on his eighteen inch laptop, "This is your new security package at the kitchen door. Now let me run it." John looking intently; it was all black then he could see the full entry, "Wow that was slow; why did it take so long to load?" Glenn looked over his shoulder, "It wasn't loading; something was in the way and then moved away; watch it again." John watched as the blackness moved left to right instead of the screen just coming on line, "Man, they are out and about again tonight."

John took out his phone and was about to hit the lighting app when Sims said, "Can you make it work from here?" Glenn looked at Sims weird, "Whatta ya think I'm doin' here." "Turn the new porch light on the highest setting, and move the lens to see the walk way up to the door." Glenn looked at Sims like he was crazy; John jumped in, "We did it this morning; turn the lens all the way right and hold it a few seconds, and it will switch modes; then you will be looking beyond the entry." Glenn did it, "Um, I think we, um what is this."

John saw what looked like a big black canvas waving in the wind by the entry, "Hit the thermal!" Glenn did, the black canvas turned various shades of dark blue, "Shit that is cold; it's at the top of the scale." John went back to the lighting app on his phone and hit, "Select all, and on" The thermal image they were looking at defrosted away. Sims pulled over, "Run it back for me!" While Sims was watching John looked around for Molly; he found her way in the back of the SUV on the floor.

Sims finished watching, "John was that how it left the windows the other night?" John was nodding; he was in the back with Molly. Glenn kept looking at the image on the screen, "So it would appear shooting them is a waste of time?" Now Sims was nodding, "We gotta catch Marko quick."

Chapter Thirty-One

9:40pm

Hart Compound

As they pulled up to the entry of Sims' house, they saw Marko parked on the street standing by his car. As Sims approached the car he noticed Marko had a 9mm by his side, "Weird shit out tonight aye Marko?" Marko relaxed, then helped Sims load the three boxes into the SUV; when he was done, "Sims, I lived by those things when I was young; obviously you know about the light, but using fire works much better; especially on those cold bastards."

Sims leaned against Marko's car, "What did you guys call them back then? Marko looked out toward the compound, "Ghosts from the sea, demons from hell, and fat black bastards; what do you call'em?" John was approaching them; Sims started walking back to the SUV, "Varmints or vermin." Marko shook his head, "Dat is some California shit right there."

John asked Marko to hold up, "Hey where do you land around here with all these hills?" Marko hesitated for a second, "Buddy of mine owns a hay farm north of here I land on his service road." John smiled and started to walk away, "Is he really big, blond hair and no neck?" Marko waved his hands like get away from me, "Oh man, oh man." He got in his car shaking his head.

John got in the SUV, "Get everything you need I think we should drive this up to the front door." Sims stuck his head in the driver's side window, "How about we use it to block the kitchen door?" "You win, that is a much better idea." Sims ran back into his house and came back out with an army issue duffle and threw in the back, "I think we might need all of these." They started up the gravel road; moving slowly with the bright lights on.

John turned to Glenn, "Can you access everything you need from the widows suite?" Glenn thought for a second, "Yes, I will start with the journals; that way we won't have to lug all the boxes up there." John looked at him, "Get it going now; we are going to throw the boxes in the kitchen and then we are heading up. Sims you double check our supplies, and I will start lining up how our friends are moving; that should give you time to get the night vision gogs ready to go."

When they had all their gear stowed in the suite and on the walk ways Glenn turned to John, "You don't need thermals to do that?" John stopped, "We have been looking for missing parts of the landscape or the holes out there." "So why not use the thermals it's a lot easier?" John stopped, "How would you suggest I do that?"

Glenn walked over took a set of gogs from Sims and pushed a blue button by the left eye lens and handed it to John, "Don't sleep during training and don't go into town!" John knew he had that coming; he turned the compound lights to normal; he slowly walked out on the east walk and put on his night vision gogs.

He fussed with them to make it comfortable, and then took a look. What he saw was a sea of various shades of blue and red; their numbers had tripled. John came back in and sat with Molly looking defeated, "Sims you were right; Molly had it figured out all along. There are three times as many; they moved in with the lights on; so they are adapting." Sims took the gogs from John and went out on the walk, *hmmm; why am I suddenly feeling like Davey Crockett.*

Sims went around the entire walk with the thermals on; he came back in and found his duffle bag and took out a phosphorous grenade and a mini launcher, "What time is it?" John looked at his watch, "10:30pm." Sims determined, "Marko said that he had lived near these things. He said light worked ok for a while; but fire worked much better."

Sims held up the launcher which looked like a sawed off shot gun, with a chopped stock, "We need to watch these guys like we planned; we need to know who is in charge. I want to know who most deserves a phosphorous grenade up his ass." Sims opened the launcher like a flare gun and inserted a grenade then slammed it shut.

John slowly sat up; a wry smile on his face, then looked at Glenn, "Phosphorous you say?" Glenn smiled, "Up his ass, you say?" Sims was beaming, "Yes, right in the ass should do; don't you think?" John stood up put on a pair of gogs, grabbed a pad of paper, "Glenn find us something on these assholes."

Glenn went to work on several problems. First, he passed out ear buds and set up communications so they could talk back and forth. Second he brought up the 3D image of the Norlander house with the proper matches from the Luedtke diary. He then overlay it on the compound; the kitchen being the registration point; it only fit with the scripted mantle over the current kitchen.

So now he needed to figure out what was so important about it? He looked in the composition book and leafed through until Teshuvah caught his eye. After he read the entire entry he got angry, *Semjaza, you're the one that has been the pain in our ass.* Then he looked at the dates, *well not you, but maybe your great grand kid.*

He quickly went through all the journal information and ruled out what he thought was hocus pocus devil shit. Then he went on to the message above the door. He looked in the journal got the scripture and entered it and did a search; as he was reading he was trying to update the visions into today's language. He tried to imagine what a stage coach driver heading west would say about a space shuttle launch.

He had it all worked out until the description of the creatures coming out of the gateway was given. He discarded that image and went on to the belching smoke and plume rising up with the creatures coming out like a swarm of locusts; like locust, not locusts because of the description of the beings.

From his modern viewpoint he was seeing news footage of F5 tornados; huge funnels and debris at the base looking like smoke as it tore along the ground; in this case not debris, but clouds of beings. The best summary explanation was the vermin they were facing are the gate keepers, making sure the way was clear for Abbadon.

Glenn activated his com, "Guys I think I got it figured out; you need to see this." John and Sims came in the suite, and removed their night vision gear. Sims went to the fridge, got everyone a beer, and sat down. John sat next to Glenn looking over his shoulder, "See what?" Molly moved from the west door to lay next to Sims' chair. He reached over got her bowl and poured some beer in it.

Glenn now talking fast; he explained the modern ground rules for interpretations of ancient visions and such; "Now based on what I have read and seen in the journals, I think these things are guarding the whole Norlander structure because this Abbadon guy is coming down like a meteor to release swarms of bad guys on the earth for five months. It may not be him that lets them out; but he is their king. That's what the script above the kitchen door says." John looked puzzled, "What bad guys?"

Glenn moved the laptop and went full screen, large text and brought up Rev 9:11, "These bad guys." John moved the laptop so he could see better; he was scanning then he slowed down to focus in on the face descriptions of hideous men with long hair, and teeth and mouths like lions; with stingers for tails; and like locust they fly in swarms. They sting men, but they do not die. They sting them over and over again, until they cry for death.

Sims sat forward; John was rubbing his chest as he was reading; there was terror in his eyes. Suddenly John jumped to his feet, "Son of a bitch; damn it; how is that even possible?" John fell back into the couch; Molly was on him in a second; John buried his face in her fur, "What in the hell is going on; what!?"

John's sudden move had startled Glenn, "Damn John what's wrong with you!" Molly squirmed to regain John's attention; he put his head on her neck again.

Sims grabbed the laptop and read it; when he got to the description, he looked over at John. He gave the laptop back to Glenn and went out on the east walk; Glenn was right behind him with the laptop, "He scared the shit out of me; what is wrong?"

Sims looked surprised, "John never told you about his dreams?" Glenn puzzled, "Yes, a long, long time ago." "Well your bad guys kill him every month." Glenn read it again, "This is not how he told it back then; this is more detailed, without the dude this and dude that."

Sims looked Glenn in the eye, "So how does this happen? Hasn't he had enough of this crap already?" Glenn was shaking his head; "Maybe John is tied to this thing; maybe they can't do shit as long as he is in charge of the Norlander house. Sims started back, "We can't be wasting time."

Sergeant Sims stuck his head inside the suite, "John you done? We need you out here right away." Molly got off and lay down near the chairs; John got up and went outside, "So, now we plan to wrestle with God?"

Sims stepped into John's space, "You don't believe that shit any more than I do; let's stick with what we know. The varmints out there are not from the Bible; not in there! This compound isn't in there either; we sure as hell aren't mentioned. But we think that if we don't do something; a lot more guys are gonna be having your dream."

John was quiet for a few seconds, "Glenn what else are we dealing with?" "Well, if these locust guys get out; they are out for five months; raising hell. "So we can keep'em from getting out, or we can try to take them out on their way back five months from now."

John looked around still a little lost, "How long we got before the storms meet up?" Glenn opened up the laptop, "I got an alarm set; constant evaluation with a countdown clock going; we got nineteen hours." John looked at Sims, "Sun down tomorrow?" Sims said, "We got to be alive to do anything; so can we burn these bastards out front now?" John held up his hand, "How many grenades you got Sarg?" Sims got his bag, "fourteen"; "How many hours until daylight?" Sims smiled, "Seven."

John put on his night vision and went on the eastern walk; turned on the thermals and saw that most of the cold spots had moved more to the south, "Sims you got your gogs on?" Sims coming out on to the walk, "Do now, what are you thinking?" John waited until Sims was standing next to him; he took out his phone and killed the lights; he faced southeast, "Can the launcher reach far enough to cut those guys off, or do we have to move?"

Chapter Thirty-Two

10:30pm

Nick's room

Rockland, Maine

Nick was hoping to hear from John; he figured Marko had made the delivery of the journals and boxes. He had been online; now he understood the journals and the scriptures on the Norlander mantle. He was wondering what John would do when he read the descriptions of the creatures that swarm out the gate. His room phone rang; there was an envelope left for him at the main desk.

Nick returned to his room and made sure there was no way anyone could see or hear him; he swept for listening devices again; sat down at the small table in his room and opened the envelope.

Gershom Scholem was the name of the man who infiltrated the compound. He was an Israeli, 26 years old, former Mos'sad; discharged via inquiry related to The Cabal and Kabbalah. Specialties were hand to hand combat; entry for capture, and surveillance.

The subject is wanted for questioning in several cases related to the disappearance of key citizens. Current where abouts unknown; last seen in Rockland, Maine 2012.

Nick finished the report then looked at the time; it was 11:30pm in Jonesborough; he called John. John picked up saying, "I'm a little busy right now; we have three times more vermin then last night; we think they all have tickets for the tornado show due to hit us at dusk tomorrow. "They are adapting to our lights and their surroundings; we have kept them out of the house so far; we are currently applying phosphorous to the ass ends of selected varmints.

"I need you to get to Confidante and get set up for the tornado. I will have Glenn contact..." John paused a second, "Glenn! Who do you want Nick to work with at Confidante? Ok good. Nick you need to work with Jacob, he is Glenn's guy on level three. Shut the company down and send everyone home except our Mil Spec security; you got that?"

Nick was confused, "What are you planning?" "We are going to video the entire tornado from the second it comes on our property until it is gone. Glenn is getting all of our cameras ganged together to get a 360 degree look. One of the cameras is bound to see them if these locust guys actually show. Also we are putting together a couple of other contingencies that will require remote access. I am hoping for sound. We will try to get to Knoxville before it hits the fan."

Nick looked down at his report; "The guy Sims killed was former Mos'sad; working for the Cabal in Israel; some spooky religious deal. I think they are Teshuvah LLC. Maybe Abbadon is the club president." John said, "Well we have to make it through the night or all of this shit is moot; so go get in position to help us. Nick? Thanks for raising me." John hung up.

Nick called Gavin Tanner immediately, "Gavin we have an emergency; John needs you to shut down the company, get everyone out of the building, keep only the Mil Spec boys, and make sure they are ready for anything. I need Jacob from level three to stay and prepare to interface with Glenn from Jonesborough; they need to max out all the video capabilities of Jonesborough and Confidante."

Gavin sat down, "This sounds bad; are John and Sims alright?" Nick being patient knowing he was coming to Gavin's company, "They think if they survive the night they can resolve this whole thing.

"There is a tornado heading right at the compound, and it is not a random event. We know now a radical group, maybe from Israel, believes that when the storm hits the compound a major religious prophesy will be fulfilled.

"We don't know if they will send people in the morning to take the compound; they may not need to; these creatures they have been dealing with are adapting to the lights that kept them away; John and Sims are using phosphorous now.

"Maybe the cult will wait until after the event; either way they want the event to take place. They need the Norlander's house to complete their fantasy."

Nick hung up and called Marko, "Allison would you like free tickets to the party in Jonesborough? We thought you would like to dance with your old friends from Rockland."

Minutes later Marko called Nick's burner, "Would you like a ride to the compound?" Nick very intense, "John doesn't know I called you, but he will need help tomorrow at first light. Sims needs another experienced man. I need you to get me to Knoxville; then join John at the compound before first light.

I know that we have put a lot miles on your plane; and you have really saved our asses. We got overtime money for you on this one; tomorrow is going to be a mess." Marko was quiet, "Are we hunting or defending?" Nick sighed with relief,

"Depends on how the night goes; John's has a couple of ideas, but hasn't shared them yet.

"Do you have any experience with explosives?" Marko went quiet again; "I spent some time with them here and there; I know the ins and outs of blowing shit up."

Nick's mind was racing, "Ok, how fast can you pick me up?" "Are you still in Rockland?" "Yup" "Ok, get to this address in an hour and tell them Allison is giving you a ride." He gave Nick directions; then Marko hung up.

Chapter Thirty-Three

Sims and John had been experimenting with the phosphorous grenades and were having some success. They were not sure, but it looked like they were burning away some of them; like dead.

On the first attempt, to cut off the cold spots circling south towards the kitchen, the grenade hit in front of the lead group and spread out some thirty feet wide and a hundred and twenty feet long. When the grenade exploded the thermal view went completely red, then came back to a bright red section; the lead group they targeted was gone.

On the next attempt they counted the cold spots in an area, and then hit them again. John turned the lights off; then when flash dissipated they could not account for many of the cold spots.

They switched thermal settings and could easily account for their activity. The heat signatures where the grenades exploded stayed red up to thirty minutes.

Sims was encouraged, as was John; but John thought maybe they weren't gone, just cooling down. Sims disagreed pointing out if that was the case they would get some type of reading warm or cold; the only way they don't get a reading is if they are not present. John pointed out that they may be present in the red areas and not dead. Sims didn't like that possibility.

Sims wanted to continue to attack until they were out of grenades; John was more inclined to save some, "Look we don't want to use all of them. We don't want to be short if they decide to charge the compound and freeze it solid; then we are really screwed; I don't want to die in a refrigerator."

Sims looked at John suspiciously, "You have other plans for some of these; fess up what's your plan." John was undecided, "Look we got to keep them out of the house and stop the locust guys from using the tornado." Sims frustrated, "So how are you going to do that?" John looked at Sims, shrugged his shoulders, and he looked away. Sims didn't like what John's body language was telling him, "Oh no! You are not thinking of doing that."

John was about to tell Sims the plan, when Glenn came out on the walk, "Are they all dead? Is that why you stopped? Glenn put on his night vision, "Geez, how long does phosphorous burn? Those patches are still hot; it is so hot I can see the heat waves with this gear; impressive."

John and Sims heads both slowly turned to look at the burned areas. It did look like heat waves, until the waves started moving just like the yellow vermin. They switched setting on the night vision back and forth; they watched stunned; it looked like they were pulling red blankets out of the burned areas and placing them away from the heat.

What happened next was totally bizarre. The yellow ones changed to dark blue; they were piling on top of the red blankets; slowly they turned dark blue as well. When they finished they went to the next burned area; they were re-acclimating the cold spots.

Sims cursing under his breath, "How long did that whole thing take?" John looked at his watch; he was silent for several seconds, "They were out of action for twenty-one minutes, from blast until re-acclimating." "So they are adapting easily now; I wonder if they will stay tomorrow throughout the day?" John turned out the lights; we need to rotate our light and dark times so the light still slows them down.

John was mumbling to himself; working something out in his head, "I say we hold onto four of the grenades; we blast the shit out of these guys with what is left; then turn on the lights, the alarms, and get some sleep." Sims cocked his head to the left, "Sleep?" "Yes, when was the last time you slept? About 23 hour ago I would guess; before you got back from Knoxville. You haven't slept since. Glenn the same thing and I finished my dreams and got five hours a day and half ago; so yes, sleep.

"Let's make a plan so we can make tomorrow count. We need the strength to carry it out." Sims looked at John, "So if we blast them all at once then they will have to scurry around for quite a while recharging; that should give us at least four hours to sleep."

John turned to Glenn, "Any chance we can get overhead thermal images from somewhere?" Glenn thought of a minute, "Let me play with some ideas; maybe ten minutes."

They went inside the suite. Sims grabbed a water, and petted Molly; she put her paw on his thigh. Sims waved at John. "I'm gonna take Molly out the back she's got to go." "Take the launcher with you and your gogs." Sims nodded in agreement, "Let's go girl."

Sims put on the night vision and switched to normal then to starlight and could see some yellow ones north of the front porch; now to thermal and could see nothing below or at either side; down the stairs they went. Sims was not used to Molly following him; she was always keen on the lead; not so much now. Molly didn't go on the grass, she used the back patio again, and then went right back up the stairs without Sims.

Sims watched Molly make it into the suite, then he decided to look around a bit. He went along the outside wall of the kitchen; he wanted to see what was going on with his SUV.

He slid his gogs back down and put them on thermal; it looked as though it was clear. He started to go around the corner when the SUV seemed to rock side to side. He froze, knelt down, and put his back to the wall. He scooted towards the car. He saw three cold spots trying to push the SUV from the door way; they were trying to clear the way for Abbadon. Sims hurried back to the widow's suite.

Glenn had been looking at the satellite tasking that was available and said they could get a full look in twelve minutes. Sims told them what was going on by the kitchen door. Glenn activated the new kitchen camera. It appeared that there was only half an SUV without the thermal imaging; with imaging, cold spots rocking an SUV.

John was grinding on something, "Sims if we start the attack do you think they all will join the effort to re-acclimate their friends, or just continue what they are doing?" "No way of telling; we can still access the entire compound using the tunnels and the carts; so what are you thinking?" "Trying to figure how to sleep and keep us split up to ensure they can't take us all at once."

Sims pointed, "We designate Glenn to isolation in shooting station 3; you stay on the alarms, in here, and I will go down the tunnels to get all the explosives I can from the machine shop; we still got a lot of time until morning.

Glenn waved his left hand in the air; directing them to come and see, "Look at this." Sims and John walked behind Glenn and looked; all of the cold spots were in the front within sixty feet of the door; they were formed in a semicircle flanking the house north and south.

Sims nodding, "Looks like they want us to leave out the back; they are using military tactics." Glenn turned his head around to glance at Sims, "What? They want to let us go?" "Yes, in situations where you don't want to expend massive amounts of time or lives to win a position; you leave the back way open for retreat; especially if you know the enemy will fight to the death if surrounded."

Unexpectedly, John began to smile; Sims looked at him, "What? Is this what you were thinking earlier?" John turned to Glenn, "Bring up the framing plans for this house." Glenn looked confused, "We just did that." "I know just do it, I am looking for something completely different."

John watched as the images came to life, "You guys let me know if it is possible to get explosive charges on all the posts of the Norlander house?" Sims put both hands on top of his head, "I knew it; you want to blow this place up." John sat down. "Glenn keep your eyes on those guys while we have a discussion here."

Sims sat down and looked at his watch, "Shit only 1:35am; four hours left." John leaned in between Sims and Glenn, "I for one will not stay in this place with that Norlander ass house on or in this property; either of you want to do that?" Sims shook his head, Glenn looked like he was gonna lose a child, "No." "Ok then let's save some money on demolition and do it ourselves; but here is the problem we can't let the locust boys get out; we have to blow the tornado off the planet!" Glenn's eyes were wide open now, "That's gonna require a lot of pop dude." Sims was smiling, "Looks like your plan is a little better now; Marko just pulled up to my house. This boy knows how to blow things up."

John stood up, "Sims, go get Marko and get anything we've got that makes everything go boom. Glenn you start making a load analysis; where to place the charges; keep in mind we can section off the tunnels to focus the blast. All the labs are bunkers, as are the tunnels. We need to make the best use of the last four phosphorous grenades, and it all has to be triggered remotely.

"You do that in shooting station 3; we've all got our phones and the monitors are everywhere; I will launch the last eight grenades, and keep them looking up here. Once ready, we will stay in place until dawn, then rally here. Sleep when you can.

"Glenn, Jacob and Confidante are ready to hear from you. Guys our plan is to blow this thing from Knoxville. We will have to start at first light to set the charges, and then get gone. If we can't get out on time, we will all hunker down with Glenn in number three, and blow it from here, and hope they get everything recorded at Confidante."

Sims looked at John, "Keep the lights on and watch the alarms; the second they go off, we will be back for you; otherwise sleep tight; no dreams tonight that's an order." Sims went out the back.

Glenn stood up, "You know it may take us all day to set the charges; we will have to blow it from here." John nodded, "I am hoping the Teshuvah boys won't come for us this morning." Glenn said, "The guy that was trying to buy the wood in 1860 was named Semjaza. The guy who tried again in 1875 was Semjaza as well; probably a relative; the point is, they really want this shit to happen. But if they don't come we're golden; if they do, we have to hold the house until we can blow it. I will use the tunnels to load more ammo and weapons in stations 2 and 3.

John smiled, "We got Marko; that's like three more guys. You, Sims and Marko, that's some serious fire power." Glenn put his hand on Johns shoulder; "When it hits the fan, get up high with your long gun and be our cover. I really don't think the vermin will be around in the morning."

"Remember to reset the alarms after I am gone." Glenn left out the back. John went to the fridge, got a beer, then filled Molly's bowl with food, and her water dish with sparkling water. He picked up Sims duffle bag and the launcher; went out on the east walk, pulled on his gogs and got to work.

Chapter Thirty-Four

3:40am

Widow's Suite

Hart Compound

John sat straight up; panic in his eyes; they darted to the control panel; the alarm light was red; not set. He literally dove and hit the armed button and it turned green; he had not turned back on the lights. He had to calm down; where is Molly? She was not in the suite; he called, she did not come. He kept calling; kept looking; he stopped dead in his tracks; his mind was racing; *they got Molly? No, No, that can't be; she is too smart; yes, and I was too stupid to set the alarms.*

John had to think; he replayed what he had done in his mind. He finished all eight of the grenades at 3:00am. Then came back in the suite, put down his gogs; Molly was on the floor next to the couch; the back door was open. *Glenn left it open; he thought I was closing it right behind him; I sat down and…what?*

John started to walk around the suite like a crazy man; he stopped; what if he just locked in a bunch of the vermin? John threw up his hands they stopped on top of his head, "Molly where are you? Molly!"

John started down the stairs; he had no night vision, or a weapon; not even his mag light. He was mentally lost, and only thinking of finding Molly. John jumped off the stairs, on to the deck; opened the kitchen door, and quickly went to Molly's corner; she was not there.

He had his hand over his mouth backing up; trying to think where she would have gone; turning to head for the kitchen doors, everything went black.

John was slammed by fear; he had never felt fear like this; it was compressing his body; now completely encased in cold; so cold. John tried to think of all the things Sims had taught him; how could he escape? Punch, kick, and claw; he could not move.

John's nose and mouth were over taken by the smell of rotting death; the taste of it gagged him; he was vomiting, but everything was suspended; smashed together in the cold; he couldn't breathe!

It was happening; he tried so hard to stop it, but it was no use; he lost all emotional control; he screamed and called for help; but only in his mind, he couldn't even move to struggle for air. John heard something crash to the floor; broken glass.

Then John felt it; like a frozen hand was reaching for his heart; he thought he heard Molly barking as he was passing out, *run Molly, run girl.* He hoped Sims and Glenn were safe; how could they be, he let them down.

Another, even more intense, wave of fear gripped him. John began seeing his dreams replay in his mind; *even while dying they come for me?* When the crescendo of the first dream came the terror increased even more; the squeezing and pressure increased on his chest.

Now, there was uncontrolled screaming, sobbing, wild endless fear, and suffocation without any movement. The second dream was greeted the same way at the end John was begging in his mind for it to end, *kill me already you have had your fun,* As the last dream began he could feel his ribs crunching ready to snap.

John got to the very ending of his last dream; the hideous men had surrounded him; their faces were showing more satisfaction then ever; John saw the tail rise up as it always did; he knew this time when it struck he was never waking up; down it came. Everything went black.

Chapter Thirty-Five

2:46am

Sims' House

Hart Compound

Sims could feel the grenade concussions and smell the phosphorous in the tunnel as he made his way to pick up Marko. Even while in his golf cart he could feel the vibrations; John was laying it on the vermin out front; he hoped the plan would work, they all needed sleep.

Sims took the middle tunnel and came up in his driveway as Marko was walking up to his door. Marko saw him and came over to Sims' cart, "Nick thought you guys needed someone to save your asses; also he needed a ride to Confidante." Sims shaking Marko's hand, "My hero, get your ass in the cart. You got a lot to teach me about blowing shit up."

Sims was filling in Marko about their progression from the compound lights to the phosphorus, "You said that fire worked better so we thought super fire should really do the job; but we still can't kill them." Marko looked surprised and a bit shaken, "They are surviving the phosphorous? That is hard to understand."

Sims told him how they had watched the hot ones reviving the cold ones after they got torched. Marko was shaking his head, "So is there a point to all this effort if we can't kill them?"

Sims filled Marko in on John's plan and the Teshuvah guys. Marko nodding his head, "So if we do this right and they will all just go away?" Sims smiled, "If we do this right they will all be blown away." Marko laughed a nervous laugh, "Ok what now?" Now we get anything we got that makes everything go boom."

Sims finally started moving towards the tunnel entrances; he handed Marko some night vision goggles and he put his on; he showed him the thermal mode and off they went to the machine shop. He noted that John had ended his attack.

Marko kept his thermals on and Sims drove slowly enough to allow them time to react if they made contact with the vermin. All appeared clear as they came to the ramp leading up to the machine shop. Marko hopped out and walked slowly up the ramp and carefully looked into the machine shop; he gave

Sims the all clear sign; Sims drove up to the entry way.

They got all the lights turned on and Sims started showing Marko around, "We keep a lot of this stuff around because we can't depend on a three man police force in Jonesborough to help us if bad guys are coming to take our people or technology.

We got the Mil Spec Group that General Jack assigned to the lower levels at Confidante, but nothing way out here. This whole place is one hundred percent off the grid we can generate more power here then is needed for the city of Knoxville."

Marko opened a large metal cabinet, "Well, well lookie here. You got all kinds of timers, switches and remote detonators; does that mean you got a bunch of the good stuff somewhere?" Sims nodded to the lower shelves. Marko stepped back, "Are those boxes of bricks?" Sims smiled, "Let's get those on the table."

Sims brought out a box of grenades, a crate of dynamite and a lot of wire. Marko put the Semtex plastic explosives on the table as well. They both went through the detonators and sorted them.

When they had everything out and organized Sims told Marko about the Norlander house and how

Glenn was working on a layout for the explosives. Marko was thinking, and then he spent some time showing Sims how to link a series of explosions in various sequences.

Sims looked at his watch, "Oh man, it's after 4:00am. Let's grab a couple of big boxes and load this stuff up so we can get back...wow you feel that? It is getting cold." Marko and Sims locked eyes; Marko grabbed a grenade and tossed one to Sims, "We gotta go now!" As Sims caught the grenade he saw movement at the entry, "Through here go, go!" They went through the doors that adjoined the maintenance shed and shut them behind them.

Marko was looking around, "Let's get behind their asses; then we can lob these into the shop. We can blow them up without killing ourselves." Sims nodded and he headed toward the ramp to get out. Marko was right behind him; he stopped a second at the exit to look back; the doors were holding.

Marko started down the ramp and decided it would take too long to run all the way to the bottom so he jumped the railing and landed on the tunnel floor. He looked back at Sims then turned to go. Sims saw Marko jump the rail and he checked to see where he was and turned to go, but he got hung up.

Marko looked like he had just stepped into a photograph of the tunnel. He was half gone when he turned to Sims, "Run!" Sims heard the sound of the grenade pin hit the cement, he looked back just a second before he left; Marko had a look on his face he would never forget; it was like he smiled at Sims to say, "Do I have a surprise for this asshole." Sims got three steps and felt the blast wave lift him, and then he hit the end of the tunnel.

Chapter Thirty-Six

4:10am

Widow's suite

Hart Compound

John slowly realized he was still thinking; he had no concept of time; it was brighter now and the smell was gone. He thought to himself, so *that's dying? Wow, where am I?* It was warmer he could feel his extremities again; he still couldn't move.

John felt himself slipping away again; he was calm; he felt no need to fight death; he was dead already. John was beginning to wonder what was next; all of a sudden he was falling faster and faster; his dreams started again, in slow motion this time.

Something was very different; after each event the characters defrosted away; replaced by the next part of the dream, and so it went until they were done, save the last act of the final dream. Having surrounded him they looked at him as if they were surprised he was there. They did not impale him; they turned and faded away.

The creature had John for seventy-seven seconds before it realized what the last dream meant. It had been feeding on John's fear; enjoying the horror in his mind when the last dream played out. It immediately spewed John out on the floor; it was as if all the creatures knew at once. In less the two seconds several of the smaller ones were laying across John's body reviving him. They realized they had made a terrible mistake. They worked together over the next twenty minutes to get him back to where he came from.

John slowly felt he was awakening to some new world; he opened his eyes. He gradually realized he was on the couch in the widow's suite. He didn't understand what was going on for a few more seconds; then his head snapped around, looking for the alarm light; it was green. He took a deep breath let it out and looked to see Molly; she was not there.

He was totally confused and disorientated. He had just died; he crossed into death; that was not another dream. He looked at his watch; He was gone for twenty minutes; he had been killed chasing Molly; how did he get back here; *was it a total freak out caused by exhaustion?*

He found his phone on the floor, "Glenn?" "Here boss, I got it all worked out; we just need the stuff from Sims and we will be ready to go." John was trying to catch up, "Where is Sims now?" "I haven't heard from him since we split up; you get any sleep?" John realized he felt great; like he had slept a week, "I'm good; I'll call Sims."

John pushed the Sims' speed dial, it just chirped over and over. He called Glenn back, "Glenn try to get Sims on the line; he is not answering; let me know what is up."

John realized all he had for a weapon was an empty grenade launcher. He called Molly again with no results; if it was not a dream, she could have died trying to save him; he was starting to lose it again; he shut it down. He decided to find Molly and Sims; no more speculation; he made a plan.

John grabbed Glenn's night vision gogs and put them in Sims' duffle; he put in a couple of waters and dog treats. He put his gogs on his forehead and started down the stairs. As he approached the bottom he slid the night vision in place and hit the thermal setting; he scanned 360 degrees and three dimensionally.

Sure enough to move, he raised the gogs, and then he turned the lights on again; the compound lit up. He went out onto the deck to the grill area, and ripped the propane tanks from under the grill station; he made sure to pull the hose connections off at the grill not at the tank. He turned, lowered the gogs again; doing a complete scan. He moved slowly to the kitchen wall and looked through the glass; nothing. He looked again with the thermal setting; still nothing; he went in.

Without even thinking, he found himself back at Molly's bed; she was not there; he spun around quickly; the creature was not there either. He went to the large knife holder on the kitchen counter and turned it around. John reached in the back and came out with a 9mm Sig Sauer. He turned the knife holder on its' side, took two clips out from the bottom, and put them in his pockets. He opened the kitchen junk drawer, found a box of wooden matches, and added those.

John turned to head for the great room when he stepped on some broken glass; he looked down; it was his favorite picture with Kat. They were on the front porch the day they moved into the compound. Molly was sitting between them; everyone was smiling and happy. He set the picture on the counter where it belonged; he thought to himself, *not a dream. I already died once today; odds are pretty good that won't happen again.*

John started toward the great room full of resolve; then he was struck by another thought, *I did die; those things brought me back. Why did they put me back on the couch? Shit my dreams; what else did they do while they were in my head?*

He decided not to go out the front door; he was going underground. He turned back to the pantry, slid the door back, and went down the elevator. He could use the spot lights on the Polaris; they were military spots used by tanks in Afghanistan; Sims had done the modification for him. It should at least slow them down. He remembered what Marko said, "Light will work for a while, but fire is better."

John stepped out of the elevator, opened the Polaris' door and got in. He froze when he heard vicious growling from behind him. He looked in the rear view mirror; it was Molly; but she was different; wild eyed, teeth snarling. John spoke her name; she got worse, barking now like she was going to go after him.

He quickly realized what he must smell like. John turned his head and smelled his shirt; it was the smell he tasted earlier. She was now closer to his head and her growling was full of intent. John carefully got his hand sanitizer out of the console; then quickly washed his hands, working hard to not move his shoulders. He kept rubbing them until they were dry and then some.

John took the back of his right hand and cautiously moved it towards her. He was imagining her ripping his hand off; he had his eyes closed, "Please little girl it's me." John felt her hot breath as she sniffed him; his whole body twitched when she licked his hand. She whined, and then jumped in the front seat.

John still moved slowly around her, "Molly, Sims?" She barked and looked down the tunnel towards Sims' house; John started the car and let it warm up as he made two trips loading the propane tanks, and the road flares from the back of the Polaris. John turned on the lights and the spot beams, even though all the lights in the tunnels were on.

Chapter Thirty-Seven

4:35am

Tunnels

Hart Compound

The tunnel was clear all the way to the three-way intersection. The left went to Sims' basement; a middle choice led to the front of Sims' house; leading up on the drive way; the right was the way to the machine shop and maintenance shed.

John stopped, let Molly out, put on her leash, and walked her to the front of the middle entrance. He tugged on her leash and she sat.

He came close on her right side and removed the leash, "Molly ready" she sat calmly waiting for a target, "Molly Sims; work it." She started sniffing the air; she went to the left and waited; then all the way to the right and waited. She walked a ways into the right tunnel then came back out excited; barking for John to get it in gear. John got in the car and followed her; she was moving fast at first, but the closer they got to the out buildings the slower she went; finally she sat and looked back at John.

John got out of the car and moved closer to Molly; she was afraid of something ahead. John patted her head, "Molly, get in the car." She went immediately. John could see a shadow about sixty yards ahead. He got in the Polaris and started rolling towards it. He stopped and used the mini joy stick on the dash to move the spot lights. John directed the right side's spot light onto the shadowed area; it revealed what looked like a body lying against the sidewall. John's heart almost stopped, he whispered, "Not Sims; can't be Sims."

John got out of the car; he was still a good thirty yards away; he reached in the back and took out his night vision gogs and put them on; he switched to thermal; the body was dark blue. John scanned all the way around the scene then got back in the car.

He drove up to the body and parked so it was behind the back of the car and slowly got out. He looked around; he was just across from the maintenance shed's access ramp. John maneuvered himself to where he could see; it was Marko, frozen solid. John looked closer to see if he could tell what might have happened before his heart was frozen; it looked like Marko's right side had been destroyed by something. He thought maybe a shotgun or explosion could have done it.

John got back in the car with his gogs on thermal; he started rolling forward again; Molly got in the back seat, "So, we are getting close little girl?"

John was trying to get his bearings as to what had happened. The maintenance shed was the last out building, and the end of the tunnel was fifty yards ahead; he could not see the end of it.

The thermal imaging was now telling a story. Parts of the tunnel's road were showing colder than before. Further ahead the walls were showing light blue and pale purple as well; he wasn't far now from the end of the tunnel. He lifted his glasses; the tunnel looked like cement should look; no dull spots yet. He moved the Polaris's spotlights all around the area ahead; he could see light glare all around.

John stopped, turned off the car and listened. He scanned all around again, *this is taking way too much time; we are gonna lose the day.* He got a propane tank out and put it on the hood of the Polaris; started the car and inched forward.

John turned to Molly, "Stay, and do not run." He honked the horn and yelled, "Sims where the hell are you? You're late!" He started rolling forward a little faster; he honked again and yelled, "Ain't got all day to blow this place; tell me something." John stopped and listened again. He heard something faint and muffled; it sounded like someone was yelling under water; but it was definitely someone trying to yell back.

John's brain was on fire with possible outcomes, he steadied himself. He started the car and was moving forward; he moved his gogs back where he could see; it was showing dark blue ahead; he could feel the temperature dropping then he had to stop. The entire tunnel opening ahead was sealed with dark blue; almost black. There was lighter blues and purples on the wall edges, there was no way around; no way through.

He yelled again, "Sims you hear me?" He barely heard Sims yell back, "Pretty hard to hear when your ears are frozen; get this asshole off of me." The cold spot was using the end of the tunnel like a refrigerator to kill Sims slowly; it was enjoying Sims' fear. Without the gogs it looked like the tunnel ended just ahead; but it was dull and putty looking; a varmint for sure.

John backed the car up about thirty feet, "Sims if you got cover get there now I'm gonna blow this smelly bastard back to hell." John told Molly to lie down in the back; he went to the propane tank on the hood and opened the propane valve.

He could smell the gas; he turned it down to a slow leak. He lit a wooden match and slowly moved it toward the hoses. John knew he was going to be blown up, or he would have a torch; they lit. He increased the flow a little so it wouldn't blow out as he drove.

John reached in the console and got the 9mm, and made sure it was set to go. He started the car and slowly moved ahead. John increased his speed a little at a time; when he was fifteen yards from the cold spot he slammed on the breaks; the tank went bouncing down the cement tunnel. John was already backing up as fast as he could. He looked back for a second and saw the tank had stopped just short of the cold spot; John was glad it hadn't blown up yet. When he stopped he was about forty yards away; it was going to be a tuff shot.

He got out of the car; and made sure Molly was down. John jumped in the cargo bed so he could use the roof as a shooting stand. He focused and pulled the trigger. The report from the 9mm in the tunnel shocked him; his ears almost exploded in his head, "Damn that's loud." John settled himself down. He had missed low and left; he had seen the bullet spark off the cement. John put the thought of the noise out of his mind; he adjusted and pulled the trigger.

John found himself holding his ears, flat on his back in the bed of the Polaris. His head ached and his ears were ringing, "Shit, I guess I hit that one Sims. Oh shit, hope I didn't kill you." John realized he was yelling as loud as he could. He could barely get to his feet. John looked through the rear window as Molly stuck her head up; she gave him the look; she was not pleased with his behavior.

John put his gogs back on; the path was clear, but with a lot of blue; he scanned all around; he jumped in car and headed towards where he heard Sims. When he was thirty feet passed the pile of varmint, he saw Sims lying on the cement, "Sims did I kill you?" Sims rolled over to look in John's direction, "What the hell was that?" John ran to him and straightened him out, "That was Tennessee barbeque." Sims was shaking uncontrollably, "Get me to the house; hot shower now." John whistled and Molly came running, "Molly save Sims." She climbed up on his chest; Sims grabbed on with both arms, "Thank you little girl."

Chapter Thirty-Eight

4:55am

Tunnels to out buildings

Hart Compound

John put Molly and Sims into the cargo bed and headed for Sims' house as fast as he could go. Sims was in the shower for about ten minutes before John went in, "You gonna live? We got about thirty-five minutes until sun up; Glenn says the storms are right on schedule. It should take us at least four hours to set the explosives without people shooting at us."

Sims came out in a robe and went into his room, "John go back to the machine shop and start loading the explosives and I'll come in a minute in the golf cart; I found timers and cellular detonators; we should be good."

John told Molly to stay with Sims; he headed back. He was thinking about where Glenn was going to put the charges when he had a flash back to the last time he was running around thinking; John refocused, slowed down and put his gogs on his forehead. He was approaching the machine shop; John stopped scanned carefully then realized he would be going up the ramp to the shop blind; he thought *temperature; let color be your guide.*

He stopped at the bottom of the ramp; for some reason he thought he sensed there were cold spots around; John shook his head and hit the Polaris spot lights and high beams. As he started up the ramp he didn't feel fear; John felt something else, it was a cautious calm. John realized he had to be careful; the whole room was a bomb.

He stopped the car at the top of the ramp. He couldn't go any farther because Sims' cart was still blocking the entrance. John got out and started to walk into the room; his brain was screaming this ain't right, but his sense of calm continued; the gogs went on. John turned the corner into the room and there were two cold spots waiting for him.

These had not blended into their environment. They were glowing with all various shades of blue and purple. John stood fast; strangely he could feel their surprise; in his mind he saw the hideous men from his dream turn and fade away; he stepped forward and yelled, "Go now!" The two cold spots vanished;

John fell backward on his ass shaking, "They left! Shit they left!" While on his ass John did some thinking. He had suspected they brought him back to life for a reason only they knew; he had gambled, hoping the two creatures in the machine shop didn't want to be scolded for eating, "The Special".

John got everything loaded up in ten minutes; double checked and scanned before he headed back. John was worried that Sims hadn't joined him; he hurried back.

This time he popped up on the drive way outside Sims' house; the fresh air was great. He had not slept in two days; he was amazed at his energy; he thought, *had a little dirt nap and now I am good to go!* He could tell daylight was not far off.

When he got closer he noticed a large black suburban parked in the drive; it had a rack of spots on top and what looked like a cow catcher on the front; it was a monster.

John found Sims gathering his stuff and talking to Hoss from the Coffee Hole; John was instantly saddened; Marko was Hoss's friend. Molly was on the couch sacked out. Sims waved for John to join them, "As we were going down the ramp, I ran all the way to the bottom; but Marko jumped the rail half way down and I guess he landed right in front of one of them.

"It was weird it was like he was stepping into a photograph of the tunnel he was half way in and he yelled run; I heard the pin of the grenade hit the cement and I turned to go. When it blew I went flying through the air. I knew I needed to land so I could get up fast; I was working that out when I guess I hit the wall at the end of the tunnel. Next thing I know, I am hearing John honking the horn, and I was freezing to death."

Hoss nodded to Sims, then turned to John, "Marko said you guys could use some help at daylight; what do ya need?" John looked at Sims, "Long gun on top of the gun shed; they would never find him up there?" Sims shook his head, "Let's put him up high and have him cover this entrance to the compound." "Nice, that's much better."

John moved closer to Hoss, "Are you alone in this, or do the other three know about your side job?" Hoss smiled. "What side job?" John patted him on his massive back as he walked by.

John pressed Glenn's speed dial and then speaker, "Glenn, are you ready for us?" Glenn sounded relieved, "Yes, I got worried, I thought I was the last one alive; hope you don't mind, the Mil Spec boys will be here any minute; we got twenty bad boys on the way." John was not opposed, "When did you call?" "I didn't, Nick called me." "How are they getting here so fast?" Nick called General Jack and he got us choppers; they will be coming through the back; we still have no thermals showing of any kind back there. They may want us to cover them somehow as they land." John heard Sims whistle, "Hoss, change of plans."

John was staring at the ground, "Thermals in the front?" Glenn, sounded optimistic, "Beginning to thin out the more day light we get." John was relieved; they couldn't handle the varmints and Teshuvah LLC at the same time. He told Glenn about Marko. Things were getting very real for all concerned.

Sims asked Hoss to help him sort out the explosives and detonators. Sims turned to John, "General Jack to the rescue." John raised his eye brows, "No way Zhang Jie will miss that." Hoss had a small grin on his face; John saw it, "Hoss care to share?" Hoss looked up, "I was told to keep an eye on you; should the opportunity arise now and then; old Jack was my C.O. in Iraq; been working for him ever since." John shaking his head, "Did Jack tell you to come here this morning?" "No Marko did; Jack told him to tell me."

Chapter Thirty-Nine

5:36am

Confidante to Jonesborough

Jacob was working with Glenn on a live feed, "It is getting better every camera you get turned toward John's house. I have the 360 degree software working; just need a couple more cameras from the north side, and we can complete full visual coverage for recording."

Glenn was doing three things at once; he spent the early morning catching up on Zhang. He was not pleased with the speed at which Zhang had picked up on what was happening at Confidante.

Secondly, he was finalizing the blast plan for the tornado. He was thinking of using the tunnels as a way to funnel the blast up through the great room and out the widow's suite. If they placed the charges right he could create his own tornado; full of fire and brimstone, or house debris.

Finally, he was working on getting sound to go with all of the images that were being fed to Confidante.

He did not want to deploy the roof turrets; turning them into satellite dishes would throw off the path of the blast. He could max out their listening capability and leave them in place.

The main sound source would be the surveillance within the house; every room had a monitor with speakers and full sound. Listening devices were in every room as well; they allowed them to access all conversations during touchy negotiations. All of this had to be directed to station 3 and then to Confidante.

Glenn patted himself on the back; the compound was off the grid entirely; if it were not they could never pull this off; the tornado would knock out power thus ending all communications.

Glenn looked at his screens it was almost full light; no thermals of the creepy kind anywhere; he zoomed out to take in more of the surrounding area; he picked up twelve red markers coming through the forest toward the house; like they were going to enter midway on the property, "Jacob are you seeing this?" "Yes, and Nick doesn't like it. He is on a line with the General; they have the same feed now in the General's office"

Glenn called the chopper commander and asked if he had sited them; he wanted to drop the troops, and then swing out for a rocket attack to thin the herd.

Glenn called John. John put him on speaker, "John we got a dozen bad guys coming from the north, looking to breach at mid property."

Sims looked at Hoss, "John was right; top of the gun shed; you will have your own snipers hide; I designed it myself." John nodded, "Ok Glenn where are the choppers?" They are on approach; their commander is going to play possum; drop the Mil Spec boys then make a wide swing like they are leaving then swoop on them with rockets."

Hoss was smiling, "Sounds like Jack." John asked, "How long do we have to get a long gun on the shed." "Four minutes max." John looked at Hoss, "Leave Sims to play with himself we got to go." Sims looking at the phone, "Glenn, send the layout; I am coming through the tunnels with everything we got; I will go over the switches and detonators with you when I am in position." Glenn signed off, and everybody got busy.

As Hoss was leaving Sims put his hand on Hoss's shoulder, "Keep them off my ass, and I will end these pricks." Hoss grinned, "Roger that."

John and Hoss took the golf cart through the tunnel to the gun shed and came up via the storage stairs;

Hoss stopped in the storage long enough to do some shopping and headed up.

John showed him the way; John went to the control panel on the east wall; he elevated the stand above the foliage and raised the bullet proof glass shield around the north side of the snipers hide.

Hoss looked around, "Not bad, got a chair?" John looked at the size of him and smiled, "I will get you one; I am thinking not a recliner?" John came back with a rustic bench from the rec-room. John also set up a laptop for him, "Here is your headset; look at the screen for your targets. You can talk to Glenn and I while listening in on the choppers; you good now?" "A little Jack Daniels would be good." John laughed, "I will tell your server she will bring it around in a bit; happy hunting big guy." Hoss unzipped his rifle case and pulled out a sniper's rifle identical to Sims'.

John was with Glenn when the choppers were about to set down. John did not like the way the targets where moving into teams of three and holding in place.

John hailed the chopper, "Be aware the targets are holding in place in threes, could be mortars set to give you a nasty welcome." We got them; we will drop the boys on the south they can work around to the west; can you start a diversion?" "We'll do our best." Hoss can you get their attention from there?"

Hoss responded, "I am dialing it in now; be nice to have a couple of phosphorous grenades and a launcher." John shaking his head, "Sims you hear that?" Sims came on, "Hoss quit being an oversized pussy and shoot their asses." "Where is that girl with my drink?"

They heard Hoss laying down fire. He hit two right off the bat; then the targets started to fan out. John heard from the choppers, "We got boots on the ground; we are starting our run." John figured another seven or eight minutes until the Mil Spec boys would be at the west gate.

He told Glenn to pull way out again; when he zoomed way back he could see three targets on the hill north west at the tree line, "Chopper One you got snipers on the tree line four hundred yards west of the compound proper." "Hoss, that is fourteen hundred for you." Hoss came back, "A little busy right now, should I take a look; would require a set up change?" "No, we may come back to you." "Chopper one can you take these guys out at the start of your run; maybe a wider sweep?" There was a few seconds of dead air, "Yup, we will come in from behind them with our thermal scope and shoot'em in the ass."

Glenn switched his monitor to the tunnels looking for Sims, "Sims did the diagram make sense?" "Yes, how are we gonna sequence the actual detonations; are we going to use any timers or just one phone call?" Glenn was looking at his list, "I am thinking of having the four phosphorus grenades lead off, then the remotes and let the rest just go when they get consumed; what do you think?"

I think that would work if the grenades were in the tunnel. They would push the whole mess up looking for air; no way to stop it then." Glenn said, "We could use the timer for the lead group; how tight can we make the area in the tunnel?"

Sims looked around and paced off a distance, "Twelve by twelve. Gonna be tight; you will have to detonate with the remote at the same time or the initial blast will disrupt the remote signal." Glenn leaning his head side to side, "Ok let's do that; no timers. The clocks ticking; we got a small war going on up here; getterdone!"

John's phone rang; "Mr. Hart I see you have access to military satellites and helicopters." John tapped Glenn and pointed to the phone; Glenn was on the com and recording in less than three seconds. "That is quite the advantage; completely unforeseen on our part. We did our checking, but we never connected you to the Army.

John didn't want to play; he had no time. "And?" The caller was set back a little, "And what?" "How did you get this number?" The caller delighted, "We found a lot more then dreams running around in your head as our servant tasted your fear Mr. Hart."

John was having trouble staying on task now, *holy shit, what else did they get?* "Why are you calling me? It seems we are both too busy to be chatting." "Oh, I wanted to ask you not to kill all my men." John looked at the phone, "Are you planning to send us a list of the ones you do want killed?"

This aggravated the caller, "Mr. Hart I left the back door open so you could leave; I held back our servants for much longer than we should have; you have the advantage now because we have been merciful; shall I repent for doing so?" "You came at all of us last night; killed our friend and you almost got the rest of us; so don't try to sell me this fair play bullshit."

Glenn was distracted for a second; he was listening to Nick on the other line; he zoomed out even more; as he did John saw another fifty or so targets in the forest about seven hundred yards behind the snipers he found earlier. John covered the phone and told Glenn to ground the choppers for now.

John still not overly worried, "I see you have approximately seventy troops within a mile of the compound; soon to be much less if I give the word." John covered the phone again; and told Glenn to hold the attack on the targets left in the woods near the fence. Glenn told Hoss to stand down.

John getting impatient, "I don't want anything to do with you; we did not ask to be involved with any of the problems you are having with your prophesy project. We didn't want to kill your man either, but coming at us that way was foolish.

The caller was silent then, "Well no real harm done, he is already back on the job. However a beautiful blond wife and daddies little girl are in town today filing a missing person's report; seems daddy has not come home. Bodies are like clothes don't you think? You need different looks for different occasions."

John trying hard not to respond to what he had just heard, "We have been tracking the storms that are due at dusk. I take it that is how you are going to pick up your buddies from the nether world; then you go through all of this crap again in five months? How exhausting; not that I give a shit one way or the other, but this is my home and you're not respecting that. I guess that is just part of being the agents of Abbadon!"

Glenn got another call from Nick; General Jack was sending a special team of twelve in from Kansas;

they would be there in two hours; they would come in the front.

"Mr. Hart, we had a deal with the broker for the Norlander's house; you cut the line and took it away from us; now our time has come and you are the keeper of the gate; there is no stopping what is going to happen this evening."

John knew it was time to end the call, "Look, let's watch this play out; then we can negotiate the five month period; maybe you pay me to tear down the house; you take the Norlander place and be on your way. You pay for the spec rebuild of the compound and my accommodations until it's completed; that kind of thing."

The caller was now very calm, "That is worth reviewing; you seem aware of what takes place when the gate is opened, yet you do not question who I am?" John was getting a little pissed, "Just the opposite Sir, I believe you have been restrained because you know who I am and what I am to you and your servants."

The caller meeker now, "We will know all when the gate is opened; if it is not then the prophecies of the Cabal will be laid in stone as truth; they say there is one who will save the unbelievers from the onset of the troubles depicted in John's writings.

He is the one who was stung a hundred times and did not cry out for death." John with attitude, "It's one hundred and fifty-four times, counting last night. You had me. I was dead; why did you bring me back?"

"We see ourselves as keepers of the end times; we must defend what is truth; and truth is revealed in many ways. Your existence proves that prophesies are not events carved in stone; but warnings to those who will hear them and change their ways; and prevent those events by their actions. If there is but one who will not beg for death, that prophesy cannot be true.

"We brought you back because we will not destroy truth. It is also true that if the gate is opened; then you are just in the way." John now looking at Glenn while making a face like, *can you believe this shit*, "Well then, we will negotiate in the morning; and if your buddies from the nether world don't get out, then you will be gone with the storm; agreed?" The caller chuckled, "Then you will have to accept who you are; good luck Mr. Hart."

John was thinking of all that was said; he noticed all the coms were quiet; then he saw Glenn looking at him shocked, "You died last night?" Nick broke in, "John what the hell are you talking about?" John now flustered, "Later with this shit; we got to get ready; I am fine now, so everyone back to work." John looked at Glenn, "What were you getting while I was distracted?"

Glenn told him about the additional team; John felt better. He opened the coms to everyone; "We have negotiated a stale mate for now; if we see any movement that looks threatening we will react to eliminate the threat; I need everyone to give your status to Glenn so we can move ahead; that includes Confidante. It is 7:10am, we need to be alive and ready at 3:00pm."

Chapter Forty

11:30pm

Beijing, China

Zhang Jie had been monitoring the events taking place at Confidante for several hours. He had called their switch board and found the company had closed to address an environmental problem. At the same time there were private military, boarding Army helicopters, heading for what should have been a wilderness area west of Jonesborough, TN.

Zhang was having trouble finding information on what Confidante really was; he knew it was a large manufacturer of disposable phones and even had a high end version coveted by many celebrities. Nothing really that should interest him; but the military angle was intriguing.

He brought up the company profile; he wanted to see the people that ran the company; the name Gavin Tanner stood out; he couldn't remember why. He ran a search program he had written that would look for Gavin Tanner's name related to every company in the United States. He found his previous employer; the largest cellular company in the United States. He couldn't understand why Tanner would leave a Vice President's job with his previous employer for a President's job at small company like Confidante; he was missing something.

He worked another half an hour and came up with Tanner's income taxes for the last four years. Bingo, he was making nine times what he was making before he moved; he was the owner; a bold move for Mr. Tanner.

His first step in growing the company would be to get new customers from new products; what could he have that would captivate the military minds of the U.S.? The cell phone industry innovations were focused on gadgets and entertainment; serious uses for this platform were dried up; or were they?

He contacted his runner and told him to get one of everything that Confidante made, and get it to him by tomorrow. He went on to the board of directors for the company, *ladies first he thought, how about Jess Williams?*

Chapter Forty-One

11:30am

Hart Compound

Earlier, when Molly began barking at him, John realized that they hadn't eaten anything in a long while. It dawned on him that he was now running a large group of people that would be hungry as well. He had called Sammy at the diner, and offered him three thousand dollars, plus the cost of food, to cater the standoff; the food was arriving now.

Hoss, now down from his hide, was seeing to it that everyone could eat without compromising their positions. He was using the rec-room as the mess hall and it was functioning perfectly; all was going well.

John saw Hoss talking to Sammy off to the side; he seemed to be helping Sammy get his story straight. Hoss knew Sammy was a really bad liar; he was to tell everyone that there was a team of contractors working at the compound and John was buying them lunch. As they were talking, Sammy's wife Bev came over, and swore the same oath; under penalty of losing John as a customer.

John walked out on the deck of the rec-room to find the satellite dishes open on shooting stations 2 and 3. He didn't like the look of that. He made Glenn a plate and returned to station 3. He let Molly join the lunch line, and found Glenn in a panic.

John waited a few seconds, "Glenn talk to me; what is happening?" Glenn looked over his shoulder, "I had set an alarm to tell me if Zhang started putting things together; well he has already been into Gavin's tax returns and is now working on Jess!"

John was jolted for a second, "What do we know for sure?" Glenn let him have it, "I know this, every member of the group is covered by an army except Jess; she is at her London facility in Canada. Her security is pretty good, but we don't have people on her 24/7."

John thought a second, "What do we have in the area?" "Nothing; the closest is Nick's team in Jersey and they lost Marko; all of Gavin's boys are here or Knoxville."

John angry, "Shit! Marko's plane is parked at Hoss's farm; how do they get to London?" John looked at Glenn, I need to know how long we have before we could expect him to try and grab her; she is one I would go after, damn!"

John left station 3 and headed for Sims. He took out his phone, "Sims where you at?" Under the great room use the kitchen lift." John grabbed some food, a beer, and three waters then headed down the elevator.

He retracted the blast wall blocking off that section, and yelled for Sims. He came crawling out from a vented area, "Oh yes, I am starving, thank God you brought me a beer." Sims attacked his food; John let him eat in peace before he told him about Jess.

Sims started to give him an update, "I have maybe two hours left of layout, and then the sequencing will take another hour, and then testing the circuits; say by 3:30pm." John sat down across from Sims, "Zhang has found Confidante; he has gone through Gavin and he is looking at Jess right now." Sims whole body stiffened, "Shit, all this noise we are making; no wonder."

John looked down, "I know you put together the London team, are they good enough to get her to Confidante, or should we do something else." Sims smiled, "Marko's older brother is on that team; he taught Marko everything he knows. He will do a great job, but we can't let him know about Marko until he gets to Confidante."

John folded his arms, "Would it be better to have the two of them drive out, then fly from somewhere else; cuz Marko's plane is at Hoss's place." Sims thought a second, "I can put this together with two calls; you wanna let me handle it?" "That's why I came down here; get her ass to safety; make the calls then get this shit done."

John very subdued, "It was supposed to be you and Marko in half the time, now we just got you." Sims looked at him, "You're doing pretty good for a dead guy. What was that like? It's probably not that different for you, right?"

John called Glenn, put him on speaker, "Figured it out yet?" Glenn was anxious, "My best guess is thirty-six hours; could be twenty- four depends if he gets a whiff of what is under Knoxville. He knows it's military either way. I hope he thinks cell tech is dead for defense; most people do." John tapped Sims on the shoulder and went back the way he came.

Sims called Jess; she picked up right away, "Are you guys ok? Are those things still around?" Sims told the truth, "No we haven't seen them for a while now. "Hey, I need you to listen to me; do you know where your go bag and exit papers are?" Jess was sounding a bit shaky, "Yes I do. Do I need them right now?" Sims calm and solid, "We have a situation; all of the attention that Confidante is getting right now has alerted Zhang Jie; he has found you and Gavin.

He knows you are part of the company, and if he finds out what is really going on below Confidante, he will want to grab someone to get information. The obvious choice would be a woman." Jess was trying to be brave, "What is the plan?"

"Your head of security Dom is going to pick you up shortly; you are going to drive into Montreal, then fly private charter to Boston. You will then drive to Teterboro Airport in New York. Afterwards you will fly private charter into Tri-Cities Airport, in Blountville, TN; and then drive to Knoxville.

"You will use a different set of ID each time you start a new leg of the plan; you good with that?" She was over whelmed, "Where will we sleep?" Sims smiled; "Time to ruff it missy; in the car. On the planes you can eat, sleep, and shower; whatever. Dom should be showing up any second; is your bag at work?" She sounded afraid now, "Yes it is."

"Do you trust Dom?" Sims firmly, "I selected your entire team; Dom is a family friend he will die for you if he has to; he is the best. You gotta go, and so do I; be safe." Sims, set down his phone; then threw a wrench across the tunnel, "What else; damn it!" He climbed back into the vent and got to work.

Chapter Forty-Two

12:30pm

London, Canada

Dom Carbone parked out front of the main offices and walked into Jess's company, JWB Technology. Dom was five foot eleven inches with black hair and brown eyes. He was one hundred seventy-five pounds, and was built like the Master Cylinder from Felix the Cat (images Master Cylinder-Felix the Cat). He had a five o'clock shadow the second he finished shaving. He looked casual in his black slacks and grey long sleeve sweater, with a white Nike Drytec golf shirt underneath. He looked like a guy picking up his girl for lunch.

He entered Jess's office all smiles; Jess was looking terrified. He had called ahead and told her the plan. They would be a couple just out to have lunch; they would go to a place close by and eat. This would allow Dom to see if they were being followed; they would eat and depending on the situation they would head straight to Montreal or they would go into London and loose the tail before they headed out.

He had her bag and other vitals picked up earlier and would be waiting in Montreal when they boarded the plane for Boston. She was not playing her part.

Dom looked at her and smiled, "We haven't even started yet; no one would have had time to track you yet; we are ahead of the curve. Should I call Sims and tell him you are not a no bullshit CEO?" She pointed at him, "You keep pissing me off and I will call Mr. Sims myself; are we clear?" Dom smiled, "So we are heading to lunch, yes?" She snatched her purse, "Yes!" She didn't think he saw the half smile she allowed herself; he logged that away.

Dom was taking it slow on the way to lunch; watching for signs of a tail. He was not sure what was going on, "I want to make sure we are not being followed so I need your help; I am going to suddenly pull over on the right. I need you to jump out and act like you spilt something on dress; blame me if you want yell scream whatever you would normally do. When I give you the eyebrows, you jump back in the car. Got it?" She looked at him strangely, "Is this a test?" "Yes, I want to test the driver I think is following us; cool?" She nodded.

Dom waited until he could see the target car in his rear view mirror; it was several cars back; then at the first open section of curb he quickly turned in, "Go! go"; She jumped out waving her hands then brushing the lower front of her dress; Dom looked around like he was embarrassed; there was no way the guy could make a move, he had to drive by.

Dom saw the guy's head snap around trying to see what they would do next; his head turned back just in time to avoid hitting the car in front of him. Dom wiggling his eye brows up and down, smiled at Jess, "Great job, now let's go." They both jumped in; Dom cut into ongoing traffic, and then across the oncoming traffic, then down a side street, and out of sight.

Dom made several evasive moves, then got on the main highway leading away from Montreal. He drove for ten minutes; then he caught a transition that took them around and heading back to Montreal. Jess looked over at Dom, "We lose them?" Dom acting confused, "What?" Oh, no we weren't being followed, I just wanted to clear the baffles so I did a Crazy Ivan." Of course, he was lying. Jess had a scowl on her face, "What the hell is a Crazy Ivan?" Dom playing on her frustration, "Well it's kinda complicated; when you're in a submarine and you think…" he stopped when he saw the look on her face, "You know like a bat turn?" She turned away and looked out the window, *Sims, how could you stick me with this asshole?*

Chapter Forty-Three

4:38 am

Beijing, China

Zhang had spent the last five hours digging; trying to find out what else could be going on at Confidante. There wasn't any new activity, and the military people never returned. He had tried everything he knew to intercept any form of communications. There was nothing on the news, or police scanners. How could someone fly Army choppers over Knoxville, and across highway 81, and no one even text about it?

He was looking to see if they had any leverage on people that Gavin Tanner had worked with. Nothing was coming up from his past employers.

Zhang smiled a wicked smile; he hated temptation; he knew it could be the end of him; but his name meant "hero" he could buck the odds. He whispered to himself like the psyco he was, "Mr. Tanner you do have a wife; now where would she be?"

His computer chimed; he came back from the window, and read the message. He picked up his coffee cup and threw it against the wall. The message read, "Lost Williams."

Chapter Forty-Four

2:45pm

Shooting Station 3

Hart Compound

Glenn pulled on John's sleeve, "Dom just checked in. He said he just did a Crazy Ivan; baffles are clear; almost to the starting line." John smiled, "Make sure Sims gets the update.

"Ok, now let's zoom way the hell out and see if the Gollum's of the Cabal are holding, and or reinforcing." Glenn backed out so they could see a mile all round; Glenn had the software scan the area. There was a small thread of red targets on the other side of the forest.

John squinting, "Fly over part of that, and zoom in." When Glenn got there it looked like a bunch of supply, or staging areas; lots of stuff, but not many actual people. John asked Glenn to check now and then for a pattern of targets rotating through the stations, "I doubt Sammy would cater for them as well; could be Phu with donuts." Glenn looked at him, "I am gonna check on Rouse's team."

Glenn came back, "Fifteen minutes out pretty much on time." John thinking things were going to turn in their favor, "Check on Sims how close we are to being ready." Glenn nodded, "We still haven't sequenced."

John's phone rang, "Mr. Hart I think you are about to break our agreement." John didn't want to talk to this asshole, he wanted to kill him, "How would I be doing that?" "There are more choppers coming our way."

"Not to worry, those are my guys coming back from Kansas. Its only twelve people, they are mostly tech and medical types." The caller sarcastically, "So I can have twelve more people as well?" Glenn stuck up his hand and mouthed, "Starting sequence now." John looked at his watch, and covered the phone, "Gotta hurry!"

John liked sarcasm, "You got a name?" "I am Semjaza, child of heaven." Glenn's head snapped up to look at John. John covered the phone, "What is it?" Glenn reminded him about the history of Teshuvah trying to get the Norlander place.

John pondered that for a second while recalling his phone call with Nick, "Well Ángel Samijazz, you didn't do well in math I take it. You still have twice the people, and a whole bunch of servants that come out at dark; so no for you, and yes my men get to come home."

"Mr. Hart please take a look at my troops north of your fence." John and Glenn panned over and zoomed in; they were confused for a bit; there were the same amount of targets all red dots right where they had been. John was about to ask what was the point, when a blue target emerged from each of the red ones; doubling the targets.

John looked at Glenn, "Can they use software to make us think they just did the whole cell division thing with their men?" Glenn shook his head, we would have picked it up right away."

John shaking his head, "Nice trick, a little Kabbalah to bolster the Cabal? The only way I can be sure that it is not a trick is to see if they burn. You ready or do we still have a deal?"

"Mr. Hart, my tricks as you call them started with our servants before the times of Jesus. Kabbalah is the greatest of the black arts." When Abbadon leads the nether world boys through the gate, make sure you stick around, he is truly a force no human has ever encountered. He will be a joy to watch.

John now hated this guy, "Black arts? Really, I don't give a shit about your religion; how many times do I have to tell you that. But, if this gate you speak of doesn't open then you and all the other Semjaza boys will have failed again.

Semjaza interrupted, "John, just for the record, I am the only Semjaza, and have been since the very beginning; though I've hardly looked like myself for the past thousand years. Your life and lives of your people are but a blink of time, and really are not important in the scheme of history." John came back at him, "Talk about a waste of time; do we still have a deal or what? The storms are not far away."

"Well, we can wait; but I seriously doubt that any of you will survive after the gates open. Abbadon and his boys will be in a very bad mood after suffering in hell for thousands of years."

John tired of this guy, "Speaking of hell; if you guys are still around after your boys are a no show, I will burn you down. You may think that I will not burn your men in the forest; I own the full two square miles your asses are parked on, and I have no problem scorching all of it." Semjaza hung up.

Rouse's team landed inside the fence on the southeast corner. Glenn was still thinking about Semjaza.

John went out to greet them and found that Hoss and Molly were directing, and getting them oriented. Molly was following Hoss to make sure he wasn't hiding food from the solders.

John introduced himself and started to ask questions; the team leader interrupted him, "Sir our orders only come from Master Sergeant Cartwright; excuse me sir." John turned and looked at Hoss; Hoss noticed he was looking, "I'll be right with you John." John thought, *Hoss Cartwright? I knew it!*

John watched as the team came together and they were briefed by Sergeant Cartwright; when they broke up the choppers took off to join the other two on the far west corner. Hoss and Molly came over, "I sent the choppers to join up with the others and determine how best to become a fast reaction strike force; check all their fuel and report the limits of their capabilities. So what's our plan John?"

John slapped Hoss on the back; "Sergeant Cartwright we need to have a chat; the asshole that runs these guys across the fence there, is really starting to piss me off." Molly was pleased they were heading back to toward the lunch line.

Chapter Forty-Five

3:15pm

iLe Perrot Private Airport

Montreal, Canada

Dom felt good about getting to the private airport without being spotted, but that didn't mean all the airports weren't being watched. They were approaching the private boarding area for their flight when Dom got an all clear from the teller in the waiting area. She worked for Marko.

They boarded the plane; Jess went straight to the ladies room, and Dom lingered around the cab area. The pilot was French Canadian and the stewardess was Korean.

The stewardess asked him to take his seat so they could get underway. Dom leaned forward, "I am waiting for someone." She was confused, "Sir everyone is here." Dom smiled seeing the new pilot and stewardess approaching; "Now everyone is here. You two are now asked to leave so we can get underway." The pilot was about to protest when he saw airport security in the doorway; they were removed, and twenty-four hours later they were released. Jess came out of the restroom none the wiser, and Dom told her to buckle up.

They had a smooth take off; the pilot disabled the transponder so no one could track them. Earlier he had entered the wrong tail number in the log, so they were gone. Dom texted Glenn; "Clean start; Big Papi here we come."

Chapter Forty-Six

7:30am

Beijing, China

Zhang Jie was running out of coffee mugs; Jess Williams had not shown up at any airport; he had spent a fortune putting people in place; and nobody had seen anything. He was now looking at surveillance cameras to see if he could spot them driving to Confidante.

He was still having trouble finding a real address for Gavin Tanner; someone had gone to great lengths to lead people a stray. All of this made him certain that Confidante was a cover for something much more important than disposable phones.

He had spent the last three hours running security on his own equipment; he didn't know of anyone on the planet that could monitor him without his knowing. He was also aware that not everyone on the planet had been accounted for. In twenty minutes the security run would be complete; then he could gamble a little to find Mr. Tanner's wife. He went to the restroom.

He had not accounted for Glenn, who was now panicking. Zhang was just minutes away from finding the real where abouts of Laura Tanner. Glenn called Nick, "Nick get Gavin to release a public statement to the media saying they are going to reopen and make up a story about some shit. Zhang is looking for Laura right now. The release will slow him down; I am going to send Sims to deal with this the second he is done; have Gavin send a car for Laura wherever she is, and get her to Confidante.

Nick took Gavin aside and told him what was going on; Gavin was calm, "Sims took us through how to deal with this; we have run it through our minds, and we have practiced our getaway; I am going to get her.

Gavin took out his phone and pushed a single button and waited; he received a text back saying, "Option one." He responded, "Taking a drive." He told Nick to write the press release and he was gone.

Zhang was staring out his window that over looked a strip mall type block that led to a worldwide chain hotel; sometimes he would use his binoculars to spy on women getting dressed; he liked the American girls; his computer chimed.

He could see his scan had found no threats or intrusions; there was an announcement from Gavin

Tanner about the Confidante situation. He brought it up and began to read.

Chapter Forty-Seven

4:15pm

Hart Compound

John was pacing in shooting station 3, they were behind schedule, "Ok Glenn what have we got left to do; I need Sims out of there now."

Glenn called Sims; Sims started talking first, "Shit! I will never get this damn thing ready with you calling my ass every second!" Glenn smiling, "I called you thirty minutes ago!" "Wow, I didn't think I slept that long." John realized what they were doing, "How long have you assholes been finished?" Sims laughing, "We just got done; so you go change your Huggies while we test the connections; you are such a whiner when you need changing."

John looked at Glenn sternly, "Well?" "I don't think you whine that much." "No are we done?" Glenn said, "John you are not yourself when you are stressed, you should eat a snickers." John finally lost it laughing."

Sims climbed out of the vent cleaned up the entire area; sealed the blast doors; then went up the elevator to the kitchen.

He looked in the fridge and found a couple of beers and a left over sandwich. He turned around to find Molly sitting pretty looking for a hand out; "Molly I haven't eaten in a long time; I know you have." She acted ashamed, but followed him anyway.

He saw Hoss and called to him. Hoss walking over, "You done already?" "I would have been done yesterday if Marko was helping." Hoss nodded, "I hear Dom is on his way." Sims took a swig of his beer, "That's what I wanted to talk to you about; can you talk to him when you see him? I got to take care of something; I am flying to Knoxville." Hoss looked away, "I can do that."

Sims stood up, "Could you have one of your boys cover me down to my house so I can shower then I need a lift to the chopper?" Hoss shook Sims hand, "John is way ahead of you; they are gonna drop you, then load up on phosphorus, and return for the barbeque." Sims laughing, "I like the sound of that. Thanks for keeping them off my ass."

John and Glenn were working on the storm track; John didn't like what he was seeing, "Are the storms moving faster? I think the arrival time was different before I got eaten by the slime servant?"

Glenn was shaking his head; "I might be crazy, but it appears the storms are getting a little faster every twenty minutes. I just ran a speed check for the last five periods, and it is now four miles per hour faster. It looks like they will meet about twenty minutes before sundown; what does that mean for us?"

They were looking at the countdown clock on one of the eight monitors in shooting station 3. John sitting down for the first time in hours, "So how much has he moved up the storms from our time estimate last night?" Glenn looked at the numbers, "The countdown clock has been automatically recalculating the time, but I did not set alarms for changes; that's my fault; let me see; Yup, same number between twenty and thirty minutes before sundown; which will be about an hour before darkness."

John popped up, "Damn! Tornados go faster the bigger they get. Check it!" Glenn went back to the laptop, "You're right they have grown to match the speed." John sat down and put his head in his hands; Glenn shook his head, "Stop doing that and tell me what is wrong." John looked up at Glenn, "If it continues to grow we may not have a large enough explosion to short circuit the tornado; it might literally be a fart in a wind storm."

Glenn's laptop beeped; his face went white. John looked over his shoulder and Glenn was ripping through screen after screen. John leaned in next to his ear, "What is it?" Glenn never looked up, "Zhang found Laura; they may have company in the next thirty minutes; depending on where she is."

Chapter Forty-Eight

4:45pm

The Commons Shopping Mall

Knoxville, TN

Laura Tanner had made it to her favorite clothing store on time; she had done her part. Now she would talk to her lady friends, grab something to try on, and hide in the dressing room.

At exactly twenty-three minutes after the call from Gavin, Laura would walk out the rear entrance of the store, open the door on the Maserati, get in, and get down until they drove into the shelter at Confidante. The shelter was a blast bunker with a special garage door type entrance that would allow for cars and crew cab trucks.

Gavin was on schedule and about five minutes from the alley behind Laura's store. He had activated the tracking on his car and could see Laura was not moving; she was in the dressing room. Gavin turned into the alley right on time. He could see Laura starting to move to the rear of the store; he needed to slow a little; as he did he saw a black Lexus coupe pull into the alley at the end of the stores in front of him; his way out was blocked. Gavin slowly passed by the alley access street on his right; he could see it was clear; if he had to back up in a hurry, he could use it as his second outlet. Gavin and Sims had worked on his evasive driving, and had power reversed passed this opening and out several times. He had just serviced the Maserati, so he was ready.

Gavin pushed a small button on his side of the console and it flipped over and was now a holstered 9mm hand gun. He looked down at the tracker, she was just about to open the door. Gavin looked in the rear view to get his bearings; another black Lexus was just entering the alley. Laura had just put her hand on the car door when Gavin saw someone coming behind her; he yelled, "Down!" Laura knelt just like Sims had taught her; she heard the gun go off; she looked over her shoulder to see an Asian man flying backwards without a face. Laura got in, got down, and yelled go. Laura prayed for her husband.

Gavin dropped the gun next to Laura and was already screaming backwards through the smoke of his tires; he was racing the Lexus to the outlet street; they were closing fast. He could tell now that he was going to win; he needed himself and the car to perform; his wife's life depended on it.

As Gavin approached his transition point he moved the car as close to the passenger's side wall of the alley as he could get without hitting the dumpsters; he could not let the Lexus get under his right side; Gavin saw the Lexus driver realize what he had done; he did not expect expert driving from a CEO.

Gavin hit his mark, slammed on the brakes, turned the wheels to the left as he put it in low, and punched it. The whole right side of the Maserati was raked with automatic weapon fire. The small arms bullet proof glass held; he was getting good separation from the Lexus.

Gavin pushed the hazard button on the dash; Nick saw it at Confidante, "Gavin is coming in hot! I want double crossers at the last two turns, go now."

Gavin had followed the route Sims had laid out; he went blasting by the police station, but no one saw them; no one followed; they were on their own.

He was coming up on the last two turns before the ramp and Confidante. He needed more separation he was up to 90mph on the side street; there was about forty yards between them, and he was pulling away. As he came to the first right turn, he slammed on the breaks and drifted into the turn, then put his foot to the floor coming out of it.

Gavin heard a huge crash behind him; the Lexus had hit a pickup carrying a load of bricks. The first crosser had got the job done; he heard Sims in his head, *you are not in the bunker yet; move it son.* They made into the bunker, the door closed and the lights came up.

Gavin reached over and helped Laura up into a seated position; she looked at him and smiled, "Shit we did it; just like we practiced; wow you were awesome…" Tears filled her eyes and she started going into shock; Nick and their EMT arrived as she started shaking.

Gavin opened his door to go around to her and he found his legs were wobbly; he held out his hand it was shaking uncontrollably. He mumbled to himself, "I need Jack Daniels." Nick pulled a half pint out of his suit coat and gave it to him; he looked in to see Laura coming back around she smiled at him. Nick turned back to see how Gavin was doing; he saw the empty bottle on the hood of the car; Gavin was smiling, staring into space. Nick called Glenn and let him know that Gavin and Laura were safe.

Chapter Forty-Nine

5:45pm

Hart Compound

Glenn called John, "John, Laura and Gavin are safe and back at Confidante we got about an hour, do you know anything yet?" John turned away from Hoss and the team leader, "We are going under the house and have the demolition specialist evaluate our plan." Glenn leaned back in his chair, "I hope our numbers are good? Have you got Molly?" John turned back, "I put her in the dream room with some water and food she was over stimulated by all the activity; she would never have stopped on her own."

John put away his phone, "So, you looked at the plans and specifications, now all you need is to look at our layout, the type of explosives we have, and you will know the blast characteristics?" Hoss said, "That shouldn't take long after he sees it; so let's get in there."

The demolition specialist's name was Sergeant Mitchell; his team members called him Mitch. He was tall and very thin, but looked strong and athletic; with short cropped light brown hair, and hazel eyes, he looked to be around twenty-seven years old. He had done two tours in Afghanistan; working to disarm IEDs as well as bringing down structures. According to Hoss the sergeant knew his stuff.

They showed him the path of the storm; the gate of Abbadon; then took him below to Sims' set up. He looked at the tunnel configuration then crawled in the vent and inspected everything; he jotted down the explosive combinations, and paths of least resistance.

Sergeant Mitch climbed out of the vent and looked at John, "Sergeant Sims put this together?" John was nervous, "Yes, with the help of Glenn Burquist." "Did you know that the geeks, like Glenn and the others, called him Sergeant Scream?" John thought for a minute; "From the book Over There?" "That is correct Sir. That is some good work in there; he is getting everything you can get out of your explosives and location.

"Give me a couple of minutes and I will have an answer for you." John was confused, "I thought you just gave me an answer?" "Sir, I said it was a damn fine job setting it up, that doesn't mean when blows it will give you what you want.

I will do the numbers, then I will tell you what is going to happen; you will smile, or you will get pissed; now let me do my thing."

They went upstairs into the kitchen; Mitch and Hoss sat at the table. John went upstairs and found Molly sleeping on his bed. She had never done that before; it always bothered her to be where he suffered; he mentally logged that away. He would chat with her about it later; *later shit, the whole house was going up in flames in an hour or so.*

John came back down to find Glenn also sitting with them at the table; he had his laptop with him. John looked at Glenn, "Is it time to leave?" Mitch looked at John, "Would you like to hear what I see this producing? You own this place, Yes?" John nodded, "I hope you got insurance?" John smiled, "I could write a check for one hundred sixty million right now; if I needed more, I would have to transfer some funds; I'm good, what ya got?" John glanced over at Hoss, "Don't tell Sammy and Bev they will raise their prices." Hoss shook his head, "Phu is going to charge you twenty dollars a cup and Molly a cover charge." John looked at Mitch, "Sorry how bad is it?"

Mitch looked at his paper, "The initial blast will send your roof and center of the house about four hundred fifty feet straight up in a tornado of fire;

sucking away all the oxygen within a one hundred yard radius.

"As the rest of the explosives are consumed, they will act accordingly; like a ground force taking out the back of the house and your rec-room over there. Now Sims house will survive and so will ninety percent of your tunnel structures. So in summary if you detonate these explosives as the tornado engulfs the house, you will choke the storm and replace all its wind with your fiery tornado; which will flame out in seven seconds."

Glenn smiled, and handed Sergeant Mitch his blast diagram, "That is exactly what we wanted." "I am impressed; you guys are some dangerous sonzabitches." John looked at Mitch, "Thank you Sergeant. What would happen if we hunkered down in station 3 out there?" "My guess, you would die from the ground forces and the concussion, but your station would need very little repair."

John lowered his head, "It is almost dark and I can feel the storm pressure building; I don't think we can make it to Knoxville right now?" Hoss looked at John, "Dinner at Sammy's; believe it or not he's got Wi-Fi." Glenn busted out laughing, "I am hungry; and I've had enough of station 3 for a life time."

John looked at Hoss, "It is time to get your men ready to leave; we will see you at Sammy's in a bit?" Hoss looked John in the eye, "Good luck to you Mr. Hart." John added, "Call sign Hawk." Hoss nodded.

Glenn called Nick, then headed to shooting station 3 to disable the house, and max the Wi-Fi; he got it done; then went to John's Polaris to wait.

John needed to fetch Molly and something from lab 1. He went down to the tunnel via the kitchen, walked across to the opposite side to the key pad, and coded himself into lab 1. He went to the smart table, put his palm on the right front corner, and it responded with a loud thump as all the drawers unlocked at once. He opened the middle drawer on the left side, and took out the two original prototype phones he and Nick had used to hack the pentagon.

John headed up to get Molly, and let her know they were going to see Sammy and Bev. John was putting on her leash when his phone rang; it was Samjaza, he decided to ignore it.

Chapter Fifty

Jess and Dom had returned the rent a car, and they were using yet another set of ID. They were looking forward to getting on a plane, and washing off the road. Dom saw his contact give him the all clear sign; they moved to the private charter section, then out to board the plane.

They climbed the stairs and greeted their pilot who asked him how their drive had gone; Jess looked at Dom suspiciously, "How did they know about our drive?" He shook his head, "Jess they are the same people who flew us into Boston; they work for Sims. You may want to learn to remember faces.

Has John scheduled you for any training at all?" Jess looked at him like he was crazy, "For what?" Dom just walked away, got a Makers Mark, and sat down; Jess was already in the ladies room.

It wasn't a long flight from New York to Blountville, Tennessee, and the Tri-Cities Airport. The drive from Tri-Cities to the compound was only twenty-six miles.

When Jess returned Dom told her about the remaining legs of their trip; he felt the last 13 miles would be the most dangerous. He explained it left less for Zhang to cover; there were only two easy accesses to Jonesborough from the Airport.

He told her she was driving on to Knoxville, and he was being diverted to the compound. She looked worried, "What should I do?" He smiled, "That would be the training Sims and John have put you through; all of this fake ID, and run around, you should be able to do yourself, and still not be late to a meeting."

She went to the stewardess and asked for some tea; she returned to another seat, and started messing with her phone."

After the plane landed at 5:30pm, they were standing on the tarmac when two silver SUVs pulled up to the plane. Dom went to the one on the left, talked to the driver, and then he waved to Jess, got in the passenger side, and left.

She was just standing there for several seconds before an attractive Mexican women came out from behind the wheel and stood by her door, "Jess are you coming?" Jess was confused by the entire situation, "Yes. Yes I am; let me get my stuff."

She looked up like her driver should be fussing over her; she got nothing in return. She picked up her two small bags and got in the passenger side. She was sitting with her bags on her lap, looking for the seat belt. Her driver took her bags, and tossed them in the back, turned around and started the car. Jess had not yet put on her seat belt. Her driver leaned over to look, "You gonna get that strapped anytime soon?" Jess was really frustrated, "I will get it, give me a second." She got it done and off they went.

Her driver made her way to the on ramp of highway 75 South and turned left. They had been driving about a minute, "My name is Trish Baltran, call sign Tbal; I work for Sims. I work with six others, and we specialize in target extraction and delivery.

"We have a twelve mile diversion, then we swing back to the 81 South, and on to Knoxville to deliver you to Nick Hart, safe and sound.

Jess turned and looked at Trish; she was five foot eight inches tall, very fit, with black, hair cut to shoulder length and brown eyes. She was wearing black Dickie slacks, a black cotton blouse, what looked like black military shoes, and a hand gun holstered on her hip.

285

After checking her out Jess sat back, "I am sorry I
was confused, Dom didn't do a very good job
explaining what was going to happen after we
landed." Trish looked in the rear view mirror,
"What did he say?" Jess was ready to girl talk Dom
to death, "He said he was being diverted to the
compound, and I would be going on to Knoxville;
and that was it."

Trish was checking her threat software in the NAV,
"Hmmm" was all that came out. Jess kept looking
at her, "Hmmm what?" "Well that is exactly what is
happening." Jess looking surprised, "He didn't tell
me anything about a separate drivers, what would be
done with my bags; anything." Trish looked at her
weird, "Why would he; it's is all part of your
training." Trish made the transition to highway 36.
It would be dark soon.

Trish's whole body language changed; she seemed
to be on high alert, "Here we go." she said under
her breath.

Jess sat up straight, and started looking around,
"What is happening?" Trish looked at her like she
was from Mars, "What the hell are you doing? Sit
still and act like nothing is going on. Obviously my
assuming you have any training at all was a big
mistake; did Sims never talk to you about all of
this?" Jess shook her head no.

Trish didn't believe her, "Do you have a go bag?"
Jess half turned, "Yes, you threw it in the back."
Trish took a deep breath, and looked at her, "Then
he told you! What is in your go bag?" Jess looked
annoyed, "Some clothes." "And?" Jess turned and
looked away.

Trish now pissed, "He told you. You just tuned it
out. Shit! Just do what I tell you, when I tell you.
Now I am on my own, without a team mate, nice!"

Trish pushed a button on the steering wheel, "This
is Tbal I have lights behind what do you see? I am
transitioning onto 354 Boones Creek Road"

Jacob at Confidante was tracking both Dom and
Trish. "This guy must have been parked; I got him
coming from nowhere". Trish looked again at her
NAV, "Can you tag him for me?"

Jacob located and locked in on the car and soon was
accessing the car's computer he got the make model
and VIN number; then he got shut out, "I was in
for a couple of seconds, then I got tossed out. So
that tells us that they knew we were looking; so we
know they know; so you will be jumped in a minute
or so.

"It is a black Lexus SUV; shadows indicate four
guys." Trish adjusted the NAV they were a half mile

back or eight seconds; she punched it, she pushed the com button, "Call hawk; call hawk."

She told Jess to get in the back and lay down; Jess moved; as she laid down, the back rest of the rear seat lowered and covered her.

Trish was gaining separation. She was hoping to make it to the intersection of highway 26, which would be Boones Creek. At this time of night it would be packed with people hitting the Wendy's and The Cracker Barrel.

Trish had about another thirty seconds to get there; she looked back they were getting real close; they figured it out. She reached under the dash by the NAV and came out with a square looking grenade. It had a textured surface that made it look an evil rubrics cube. Trish lowered her window; pressed the top center square; it lit up green and flashing.

Trish put it in her left hand, and put her arm out the window. She tossed it straight up in the air; when it came down, it exploded in midair level with the chase car's wind shield. The explosion was a bright flash of light that blinded everyone in the SUV. It swerved, and then spun around; ending with two wheels on the left hand shoulder of the road; ass end toward Trish.

Trish decided to take them on right there; she was still on the sparsely populated side of highway 26. She hit the overhead light with the palm of her hand, and it lowered down revealing a Mac 14 rifle; she turned the car across the two lanes and shut it down; she grabbed the Mac 14 turned on her flashers. Trish pushed the com button one more time, "Hawk God damn it, where are you?" She jumped out of the car and stepped around to the passenger side. She took inventory, three clips for the Mac, and four clips for her 9mm; she made sure the Mac was on single shot, and used the hood to steady her aim.

The first guy out was from the rear passenger side door; he seem shocked to see her SUV across the road; he was more surprised when he was shot in the throat then in the chest. The others used the rear doors as cover while they came out the passenger side front door. They set up behind the front doors, and were shooting around the through the rear door windows.

For the first ten seconds, they laid down heavy fire on Trish's position; she rode it out. She popped up and responded with five shots of her own; she just missed one guy's head, but got glass in his face; she hoped he was down.

This time only two guys came up to volley back. Trish anticipated when they would stop; she caught one guy exposed, and put him down; then the whole world exploded, she felt a hot poker in her right chest; she saw the Lexus SUV explode and smiled, "about fucking time Hawk!" Trish turned to look at the chopper, but didn't make the full turn; down she went.

Jess was shaking from the noise and rounds hitting the SUV; then there was an explosion that shook the entire vehicle; she thought her eardrums had ruptured. She believed she was deaf until she heard the chopper landing; she stayed put; Trish had not told her to move.

Jess heard voices; a man called for Sergeant Mitchell; she was relieved. She worked her way out of the SUV; it was almost dark. She saw the chopper had its flood lights pointing at the car that was chasing them; there was not much left of it; and she couldn't see Trish.

Sergeant Mitchell had rushed to Trish; Hoss took his pump shotgun and moved towards the wreckage of the Lexus. He saw one of Zhang's guy rolled over; Hoss shot him in the chest; he rolled back. All of Zhangs guys were dead; he examined them and shook his head, "Damn! That girl can shoot. He heard Mitch yell to the pilot who was standing about thirty feet away, "Get me some pliers." Hoss moved that way; he looked out into the sky; he could see the storm had just passed over Jonesborough, *here comes Abbadon.*

Sergeant Mitchell had opened Trish's blouse; he was encouraged at finding a bullet proof vest; an expensive one. Mitch thought of Sims; a hand with pliers appeared at the end of his nose. He handed his flashlight to Hoss, "Can you see it?" "I can see the hole." "That's what I meant; went all the way through; special rounds; assholes."

Mitch took out his knife and cut the straps off the vest and carefully peeled it back; it snagged; both Hoss and Mitch smiled; He pulled it back a little further reached under the vest with the pliers, stabilized the bullet, and pulled away the vest. There was a quarter of an inch of bullet still showing above her skin; three inches left of from her sternum, and two inches above her bra.

Hoss leaned in, "Nice, she should thank John and Sims she's alive." Mitch looked up, "Why John?" Hoss rubbed his thumb across his first two fingers, "John's got the cash and he spends it wisely; don't you think?"

Mitch was about to comment when Trish woke up swinging and cussing, "Where is she; where the hell is Jess?" She looked over Mitch's right shoulder; she saw Jess standing back a ways, "Ok. You ok?" Jess nodded. Mitch pushed her back down, "Trish can you see all that lightning south of Boones' Creek?" She turned her head, Mitch ripped out the bullet; she punched him between the eyes; everyone laughed and apologized.

Chapter Fifty-One

6:10pm

Sammy's Diner

West of Jonesborough

John was driving the Polaris, Glenn was next to him, and Molly was in the back staring at Glenn; she wanted her seat back. Glenn was following the storms; "He slowed it down even more; they are now just entering the property." John had a thought, "Quick check for targets; anything at all; way out and in." Glenn looked all around and checked the software follow up, "Just one; standing on your front steps; does he think he is going to shake all the boys hands and welcome them aboard." John smiled, "He is an arrogant bastard; he thinks he owns the place now." John made the last turn.

It was dinner time, so he had to park across the street from the diner at the Coffee Hole. He received a text telling him "Hawk to the rescue was needed. Performed as expected; Jess is safe; no one lost."

John waved to Phu and they went into the diner; Sammy nodded to the back; the diner was pretty busy; they had people at eleven of the twelve tables in the main room.

The back room was set up with two long conference tables, coffee, beer on ice, and lots of power strips. John turned and thanked Sammy. Sammy didn't know that all of the equipment they carried never needed charging, a plug, or ever lacked for a signal.

Glenn sat down in the middle of the table; then stood and started to go back to the Polaris; John waved him off, "I got it." Molly was greeting all the customers and making sure they were eating the proper foods. John came back in with a large monitor.

Glenn was getting excited; John shut the drape to the back room and turned off most of the lights, "Jess is safe; having the choppers in the area of Boones Creek was a good call." Glenn nodded, "Thanks."

The monitors were all up; with full sound and they could see everything. John called Nick, "Here we go. Is General Jack set up?" Nick sounded tired; they had been through it with Gavin and Laura, "Yes and Jacob is getting good video; is it time to hit the lights?"

Glenn was waiting for the storms to start rotating; the cold rain storm had slammed into the heated thunder and lightning of the gulf storm; and things started getting crazy. The storms rose way up into the night and formed a huge thunder head; it got larger and larger; John asked, "Fart in a wind storm?" Glenn shook his head no, and handed John a headset, "Put this on; you can hear and we can talk." John put it on, "Wow, good sound; sounds like a freight train coming."

Glenn turned on the compound lights, and zoomed out the video to take in a wide angle, with the kitchen in the center focus. He hit a few more keys, and John could see Jacobs input of the 360 degree view with a higher wider view; looking in from the south to the kitchen. Another view was out more, and picked up over half of the tornado.

Glenn did one more adjustment, and another screen was filled with the satellite view with thermal; the red dot was still on the front steps; impossible.

"We should be getting close" John said. They could see the compound beginning to rock back and forth from the wind; Glenn looked at John, "We are close."

John was looking up at the overhead view; he pointed and Glenn looked up. What looked like a missile came into view; like it had been shot from the camera; it went right through the storm, and into the kitchen area. "Son of a bitch; what was that?" Glenn yelled into the com.

John stood up, "Detonate now!" Glenn reached over to push the return key on the laptop, when their headsets were filled with hideous, ungodly, and blood curdling screaming. It sounded like a million people were being burned alive at the same time.

The agony of the screams ripped into their hearts; they were both repulsed, and heart broken in a second; tears came streaming from their eyes. Glenn fell back and on to the floor holding his ears, ripping the head set off; but sound was still as loud; he could still hear it. John recovered, and hit the button; all the monitors went white for a second; then they were filled with fire and the sound of the explosion. The screaming had stopped.

John was walking toward the far right corner of the room. Molly was running to him; they had been through this before; this was John's first dream. People screaming and reaching for him; trying to pull him in; they were burning in a sea of fire; he was in a small boat floating through the fire and blood. John collapsed in the corner and Molly climbed in his lap.

Glenn was crawling back to look at the monitors; both tornados were gone, and so was John's house.

The Norlander house was nowhere to be seen. Glenn went to see where John had gone, when he heard crying and groaning in the other room.

He went and pulled back the drape; Sammy was holding Bev in his arms they were both crying uncontrollably. Everyone in the diner was groaning, crying, and asking what had happened. Some of the people where curled up, rocking like they were in shock. Glenn realized he had been shaking the whole time; he found John holding Molly with both arms around her; she was licking away his tears and softly whining.

Glenn went back, and fell into his chair trying to figure what had happened. Had he pulled the headset out of its plug and all the sound came out the monitors? He looked, it was still in there.

He grabbed his head set and put it back on; he heard Jacob yelling over the line, "What was that? Glenn what was that horrible screaming; are you guys alright?" Glenn realized Jacob was crying while he was screaming into the com.

Glenn figured out what had happened, the gate had opened for just a few seconds before the blast. Millions of people were actually burning and screaming. They had heard them six miles away; like they were burning right there in the room.

John's phone started ringing; Glenn moved to his right and picked it up, it was Hoss, "John what the hell? Was all that wailing and screaming coming from the compound? We felt the blast; did those things get out?"

Glenn explained to him what he felt happened. He started looking for signs of life while Hoss stayed on the phone, "Hoss I don't see any signs of life; I think the only thing that explains the sound was that the gate opened for around four seconds and then got blown back to hell; literally. Where are you calling from?"

"We are sitting in the Wendy's in Boones Creek; those sounds I would say have screwed us up for life. Everyone for miles in each direction never wants to hear that shit again; myself included." Hoss signed off.

Nick called on Glenn's phone, "What is going on with you guys? Where is my brother?" "He is in the corner with Molly." Nick let out a sigh, "Shit I didn't think of that, he said in his first dream it was the screaming of the people that jolts him awake; this shit might really send him over the edge. Look, when he comes around tell him to get back to the compound; General Rouse is mobilizing several teams to investigate this; I guess his sound system was better than ours; he is really freaked out and wants to isolate whatever went on over there.

We still can't get Laura back to reality; she is in shock. The local news reports everybody within a six to ten mile radius heard that shit; we have to contain this; get John up and going."

Glenn realized he and John were on their own, "I hope you got all of this; we need to find that Teshuvah guy and wring him out." Nick laughed, "That asshole was still standing on the steps when the blast went off; he was vaporized." Glenn let out a deep breath, "I am not so sure; that guy is super creepy."

Chapter Fifty-Two

7:30 pm

Hart Compound

Aftermath

John and Glenn pulled into Sims' driveway and killed the lights. It was eerie to see all the lights on and no compound in the distance; just small pieces of everything, everywhere. They drove up to the south side of the site where several military vehicles were parked; transports, trucks and what looked like General Rouse's car.

As they got out of the Polaris they could feel the heat coming from the blast area; Rouse was standing near where the kitchen was. Molly was going crazy smelling everything; she was working the ground. John let her do her thing; she had been cooped up too long. Glenn headed to shooting station 3 to check it out; as he passed station 1 he looked back; only the steps remained of the gun shed.

John went over to Rouse and shook his hand; they were quiet; they had both been broken by the screaming they had heard. They were like soldiers who had suffered the terror of heavy losses and were reviewing the field of battle.

Rouse told John that he had spent his early morning on the phone with the Joint Chiefs and the Governor of Tennessee; they included local law enforcement and the State Troopers. They were made aware of a possible attack on one of our black sites. The objective was highly classified prototype equipment that was vital to national security.

Rouse turned to John, "They all agreed to stand down for the day, and filter any incident reports through my office. Even with that Zhang acted on his guess of what Confidante might be. Your guys did a hell of a job keeping him from making today even worse."

Rouse pointed to where the eleven targets had been, "I have our best trackers and recon guys out there looking for signs of movement; if someone took a leak out there they will know it. John told him how the targets had doubled on the screen.

They continued around the scene; John asked if they knew about the troops in the forest west of the compound; the general said he had reviewed the Confidante recordings on his way over; he had mapped the threats and movements with his team leaders.

They finished their walk through and Rouse faced John; "This was connected to your dreams?" John looked back; "A lot of what I have dreamed has played out; the last part with the screams; I don't think that if I hadn't heard that over a hundred times, I could have pushed the detonator. Hearing it as loud as it was, and being awake; took me out; I was down; Molly brought me back.

He turned to see where she was; he couldn't see her. General Rouse looked around, "What are you looking for?" John called Molly; then again; he heard her bark; it was her alert bark; she had found something.

John and Rouse moved toward her; she was sitting down in front of something. Her head went down to it, then back to John and she barked twice; she turned back to look at John, "Molly release." She moved away and took a position behind John. The General took out his flash light and pointed it at the area; it was part of a face.

The face was the right side of a head, with the right forehead and eye; but without the nose and with three quarters of a mouth and chin. From the forehead region was long scraggly hair and the mouth was full of what looked like the teeth of some beast.

John jumped back, looked at General Rouse and started shaking; "This is the shit I was talking about. Look at this; how many of these things got out?" Rouse took him by the arm and led him away; Molly was circling him; Rouse shook him, "None, you smoked all of them; the rest couldn't go anywhere; you slammed the door in their faces. We have zero evidence of life."

John looked at him, "That's because they have been dead for thousands of years; that's if you believe all the stuff; but hey there's a head of one over there; so what the hell."

John was crashing from the stress of the last four days. Rouse and Molly took him to Sims' house. Rouse had the medic check him out. Later, Rouse told the medic to put him out for the evening; he did.

Glenn took the Polaris down to Sims' and fixed the place up. He made sure there was food for breakfast. Amazingly enough everything in Sims' house was working; just like he had designed.

Rouse left guards all around the compound as they continued working through the night. In the morning when they let Molly out and all of Rouse's men were gone; the air smelled burnt. The General left John a message; he was to have all of his crew at the pentagon to be debriefed in three days

Chapter Fifty-Three

Midnight

Beijing China,

28 hours after detonation.

Zhang Jie had been extremely upset with the events of the last thirty-six hours. He had lost three men trying to kidnap Laura Tanner; and four men trying to capture Jess Williams. The Tanners defeated him without outside help; they had out drove and out smarted his men.

Jess Williams was being transported by a female driver, who when attacked, turned the tables on his men. She gunned them down in the middle of the highway; four against one. Williams was collected by helicopter and disappeared. The worst part was, not one police or federal officer was involved and not one word on the network news.

Zhang was proud of his personal discipline; he never shared what he was doing until he had done it; his handlers just waited for his next surprise; so his failures would not be detected. He knew they would regroup at Confidante; he had to devise a plan; once they had let their guard down, he would boldly strike.

Tonight he would relax and enjoy himself. He had already had a few drinks and a couple of hits of opium; he was the hero; tomorrow would be better.

He opened his drapes, found his binoculars, selected night, and started looking for ladies undressing; better yet a couple doing it; he was getting excited with anticipation.

He started looking at eye level, or the fifth floor of the hotel. He thought he was going to be disappointed when the living room light came on in the room directly across from him.

As the women moved around turning on the lights she was removing more and more clothing. When she was naked from the waist up she moved toward the balcony sliding door; she stood looking out without a care in the world.

Zhang thought he saw something on the next balcony over and moved to look; he saw what looked like a pile of laundry on the deck. He lowered his binoculars to get a look.

Sims saw Zhang lower the glasses and pulled the trigger; there was hardly a sound. Zhang's window exploded to reveal Zhang had a third nostril. The back of his head was on the wall across the apartment; he crumpled hitting his head on the corner of his desk. His computer had a message flashing on the screen, "hard drive formatting; don't remove plug or turn off power." Sims spoke into his com, "Hero is Zero."

Sims went back into his room; he disassembled his travel kit. Nick had sent Sims' wardrobe ahead to his room. It was a five foot tall, three foot wide and two foot deep antique, cherry wood travel closet; and so much more.

The rifle's scope broke down into four different lenses which fit the Nicon cameras in the video storage area. The barrel became the clothes hanger pole; all evidence had been chemically cleaned away.

The gun stock was wiped down and returned to lower front of the wardrobe; now it had all its feet. He hung up the shirts he had placed on the bed earlier; then he fit the ammo clip into a video camera. The bolt was an ornamental lock for the middle back jewelry doors. Should Sims ever have to stay for any period of time; clothing and shoes were included.

Sims changed out of his paper coveralls, went next door, paid the model, and sent her on her way. He put the coveralls, gloves, chemical sanitizer, wipes and unused bullets, along with a hotel ashtray into a pre-paid Fed-X express box and sealed it up. He double checked the room and headed out the door. In the lobby he visited the Fed-X drop box; then walked out the front and climbed into an SUV.

Sims took out his phone and texted Glenn; Glenn had already wiped Zhang's hard drives; and he had sprinkled enough of the right bread crumbs to lead the Chinese to the Russian Matvey; forty-five minutes later Sims was seated in first class; ready for takeoff.

When the seat belt light went off, he ordered a beer and called Kat in Prague; she needed to know what had been going on with John.

He spent quite a while telling her about the last few days; she was going to be home by the middle of next week; they worked out a way that it wouldn't look like she was coming home to rescue John, that was Molly's job.

Chapter Fifty-Four

8:30 am

General Rouse's Office

The Pentagon

General Rouse was waiting on Nick, he was several minutes late. Those present were still emotionally raw from the other night's events.

Nick finally showed up; as he walked passed John he leaned in, "I got the ashtray I sent away for; it's really a nice one. It will fit nicely with the others." Once everyone was seated Rouse made sure they felt fit enough to be debriefed.

"First the targets to the north, Hoss you shot two of the targets; what did you see through the scope?" Hoss said, "Average height, slender, and quick targets, both male wearing the same type camouflage as the intruder Sims shot." He turned to Glenn, "You found listening and transmission devises correct?" Glenn nodded; Jack pulled a clear bag from his brief case, "These?" Glenn nodded again.

Rouse stood up, and brought a box and a folder over from his desk. "John you don't have to look at this stuff if you don't want to. We found this stuff in our search after the blast."

Rouse pulled out clear bags containing fragments of teeth, hooves, hair, bones, and a finger that was about nine inches long, with talon claw type nail; when it was placed on the table John got up and walked away.

"All of this stuff matches the descriptions in the scriptures referenced on the Norlander house. We also have all of the iron wood that made up the house, widow's walk and the entire gate. John gave us instructions what to do with it.

John came back to the table, "The scripture that Tashuvah LLC was referencing was Revelations 9:1-11. I thought it would be nice to cut that shit into nine hundred and eleven pieces, approximately seven inches each, and then drop the pieces into rain forests all over the planet." Nick and Glenn really liked that idea. Rouse noted they had already cut up half of it and planes would be dropping it throughout the month.

"Now for our findings; first, there are no DNA matches for any of the samples that we collected. No species, no reference at all; they look almost common, but they are not from around here.

Secondly, our best scouts and trackers could find no evidence anyone having been shot on the north side; in fact they say there is no evidence that anything man or beast had been in that area in at least a year.

They went through the forest using the data logs from the choppers; they stood in the exact locations where the three snipers set up. There was not even a broken blade of grass; no human or large animal had been in those trees in quite a while. In fact, despite the testimony of some of the best military people we know, we must conclude the threats outside of the compound were false bogeys.

On the other hand, the entities you faced, within the compound and in the tunnels, left plenty of evidence; including Marko's body. These creatures are also not from around here. The NSA is working on finding some kind of historical match.

Using the video evidence, which you all have seen, we know that the hotter and smaller of the creatures covered the entire house to shield it; then the colder spots, or larger ones, went toward gate climbing over the hotter ones; they all went up in the blast.

The NSA has allowed us to look at one of their photo extractions. They made it using an image layering type of program; they isolated this image near the top of the kitchen door, about ten seconds before the blast. It will speak for itself.

He handed everyone a copy. They were transfixed by the image; nobody looked away; each one not believing what they were seeing. It showed a huge hand, grossly gray and scabby, with talon claws for finger nails; in the hand was a large ornate key.

Rouse reached in the box and quickly dropped the nine inch finger back on the table; they all reared back in their chairs. The General leaned over the table and pointed at the photo, "So, who the hell is this?"

Glenn hoarsely, hardly speaking, "Abbadon?"

Epilogue

Six Months Later

John hadn't had one of his dreams since he died during the attacks on the compound; good thing because the Ming chamber pot was vaporized in the explosion. Kat and Molly sensed John's tortured days were behind him.

John, Kat and Molly had stayed with Sims until they found a really nice cabin. It was above their favorite town with no name. The drive way was a mile long road; both the cabin and the road were cut into the forest. They all loved it and decided to keep it as their private getaway after the compound rebuild.

John and Kat had a great time shopping to replace all his clothes and all the stuff needed to give the cabin a woman's touch; including more feminine bowls for Molly and some cool doggie neck-kerchiefs.

John had felt guilty for all the problems the explosion had caused Jonesborough, and the surrounding area. He set up building funds to help the city maintain their historical structures, and made several small business grants in various towns nearby.

John set up a trust for Marko's entire family; they would never want for anything. Dom, Marko's older brother took Marko's place with the recently reorganized security teams. With General Rouse's permission Hoss would get Dom squared away, and make sure Marko's jet was back in action.

John bought Hoss a new harvesting machine that cost over a million dollars. When Hoss objected, John pointed out that a machine like that could service a lot of farms in the area at no charge. Hoss relented, seeing the wisdom of small farms pooling their resources.

The attacks from Zhang were the main reason the security teams needed reorganizing. It brought the realization that women needed a different kind of training; from a female instructor.

Sims put Trish Baltran in charge of the London facility, as well as maintaining a training rotation with Kat, Laura and Jess. They would all meet monthly to update their threat assessments with Glenn and Sims; then reinforce or modify the training as required. Of course they would not be training at night, which allowed for some serious ladies nights out.

One of John's final items on the punch list, was having Nick close the loop with Annabel Gibson. He was giving her all of the items they collected from Rockland. She received all of the building files, and photos, along with copies of the standoff audio, the video of the storm and explosion.

Without the NSA's photo she would not know about the hand and the key. Her job would be to finally explain, and put to an end, the legend of the Ghosts of Jameson's point.

Nick had arranged for her to sit with one of the country's top publishing firms to flesh out a fiction novel, based on the events of the four days at Jonesborough.

John also spent a lot of time with the people at the diner in the aftermath of the attack. He tried to explain what happened; they were gracious and forgave him everything. In getting to know the people; he kept asking why they had not wanted to name their little community; they would smile then move on.

John got the same kind of reactions when he brought up Adam, Hoss, Lil' Joe and Phu in connections to the TV show Bonanza. Each and every person he brought it up to looked at him like they had never heard of the show, or those characters. John knew that the entire town with no name was in on it, and they were laughing at him in secret.

One night after they finished dinner, John took Molly for her walk; Bev came and sat down with Kat. They were chatting and reflecting on how much better John had been doing since she got home.

Out of nowhere Bev leaned in and whispered; "John keeps asking why the town doesn't have a name?" Kat whispered back, "And why is it that apparently no one has ever heard of the TV show Bonanza!" Bev ignored the comment.

She kept looking for John as she continued, "This town started with Hoss and Sammy back from the wars. They wanted to find a quiet place without any political or social bullshit." Kat nodded, "So where is everyone else?" "You see the lot of them every night you come to the diner, or for coffee early at the Hole; that's all of them. We get a rash of outsiders on the weekends cuz Sammy's cooking is so good; not to mention my pie."

They laughed and Kat asked, "What do these people do? Where do they work?" Bev looked at Kat and smiled, "They all have, or have had, side jobs like Hoss and Marko." Kat sat back in the booth, "My God, that is insane. Should we tell John?"

Bev folded her hands on the table, "The people in this town really like you guys, not as much as Molly of course, but they want the opportunity to watch John discover each one of us." Kat was nodding, and then her eyes lit up, "Us?" Bev stood and went to the door, and greeted Miss Molly; then took her to see Sammy.

They went back to Sims' and cleaned up the place. Sims was due home late that evening. John wanted to take some time and go into the labs to test some equipment. Glenn had said that all power was restored to the lower level. It was secured and ready for construction to begin on the next two floors. Kat and Molly preferred a nap scenario.

As he pulled up to lab 1 he saw his Polaris; it had been cleaned up and was looking good. John hadn't driven it since he returned to the compound that last night; Glenn said he would take care of it.

John opened the driver's side door and looked in. He sat down and swung his right leg in, "Oh no!" He quickly looked in the console; the 9mm wasn't there, but his old phone was; it was flashing; there were two messages.

He took out the phone thinking Sims or Glenn had checked on him; then he remembered the first message would be from the now dead Semjaza. He looked at his messages they were both from him, *persistent prick.*

John started the first message, "Mr. Hart I was hoping to say good-bye to you, but it seems you have fled to safety earlier than I expected; that is probably for the best. Good for you to not jeopardize your friends lives; the nether world boys do get crazy, as you know all too well. Hopefully this will be the end of our dealings; sleep well John."

John was shaken by hearing that voice again. John was looking at the second message; thinking about what he had just heard. He was about to start it when he noticed the message was sent the day after the blast; another chill went down his spine.

John hesitated; he thought about Semjaza's comments about him being the only Semjaza, and having been around for thousands of years. John was now confused and very apprehensive, "Mr. Hart, you really surprised me; I did not think you would blow up your own house. I misjudged your level of conviction. Good job John; you have proven the ancient prophets correct; you have prevented the start of the Days of Woe."

Semjaza with anger, "As for me, I would kill you right now for what you have done to my legacy. I will have to pay a great price because of you. Ah, but my killing you is just wishful thinking; I am forbidden; besides there is no way to kill the truth; and truth never dies. It is equally wishful to think there could be a world without evil.

"John, I have something for you to ponder. Thousands of my servants are missing, they have scattered to the ends of the earth. They will join the others that wonder aimlessly in the night; waiting in the dark; hungry for fear.

"Let me ask you to think back, have you ever been frightened, walking home late on a warm night, and suddenly you passed through a cold spot of air? Only to go back, and never find that spot again? You ever wonder about that John?"

John shook with a chill as he remembered how it felt when he walked through the cold spot; how he was frightened and hurried away. He knew how cold they really were. He didn't respond to either message.

He left his golf cart and fired up the Polaris; he turned around and headed back to Sims'; it was starting to get dark. When he got back he watered Molly, and they all watched TV, followed by a late snack. John watched the local news; he was the last one to bed. Even Molly did not hear Sims come home.

They slept in until Molly needed to go; as John and Molly came out of their room they smelled bacon. They continued down the stairs; John was about to trash talk Sims when he saw Jess standing by the sink. She was wearing one of Sims' long sleeve shirts and a pair of socks.

John had to work hard to keep Molly from rushing the bacon. Jess acted very cool, "How do you guys like your eggs?" John was now dragging Molly to the front door, "Like my brains are right now, scrambled." She grinned at him, "Don't worry boss; I am not over easy."

Author's Note

I really hope you enjoyed this book. I would like you to share your comments with me and would invite you spread the word by writing a review at one of the places listed below.

I am a stranger to self-publishing, having only experiencing the traditional method of getting a book out to the public. I do understand that word of mouth and the written review is the engine that drives the market in today's environment. Again, it would great to hear from you and thank you for picking up the book.

Reviews

Paperback: Amazon.com and E-Book: Amazon Kindle. You can find me on Face Book at Lou Berthelson or ColdSpot11@outlook.com. I also am involved on Goodreads.com.